Author – Roselyn Dawn

Rose was born in Lincolnshire to a military whilst she was just a baby. Living abroad may have been what has caused her to be a traveller, living and visiting many different places throughout the world.

Rose is an avid reader, who loves life and all that it can offer. She loves the Spirit World and is very tuned in to psychic activity, thus drawing her to the paranormal and the writing of this book, the first of many to come.

To Phil

Best wishes

love Rose Dawn

xxx

The Linking of Souls

Preface

       Belinda followed the paramedics close behind as they lifted the stretcher into the ambulance. She moved up the steps, her heart beating faster with each step and sat immediately besides Colin as they set off for the hospital. She listened to the siren of the ambulance waling and screeching above her like the bellows of a scream as they pulled away from their apartment. The paramedics were trying frantically to keep Colin from slipping away, inserting needles into his arms, which pumped liquid into his body trying in a desperate attempt to revitalise him. Belinda's heart was pounding so fast and hard that she felt sick to her stomach as nausea threatened to rush up into her throat. Taking a deep breath and clutching the sides of her seat, she turned her eyes towards Colin's face seeing that he was unconscious. At least he isn't hurting or in any pain and even though that thought should have been a consolation, it wasn't.
"What's happening to him?" she shouted to the paramedics above the sound of the siren as it lapped over her voice.
"We don't know yet love, just try to stay calm, we're doing everything that we can," one of the paramedics replied as the other listened to Colin's heart with a stethoscope. Belinda leaned back against the seat and gently closed her eyes as the tears flowed down her cheeks and even though she couldn't hear the sobs that flowed from her throat, they were there. As she opened her eyes, she saw one of the paramedics talking to Colin, looking towards him she saw that he was trying to say something. Upon hearing Belinda shout his name, he turned his head slightly to look at her and raised his hand as she leant forwards to grasp it, holding on for dear life. She controlled and ebbed the rest of the tears that wanted to pour, taking a deep breath once again as she fought hard not to let her blurred vision stop her from seeing her beloved husband's face. Smiling at him was the hardest thing that she had ever done, as the muscles in her mouth didn't want to work, but she managed to gain control of herself for his sake.
"I love you," she mouthed, as she knew he wouldn't be able to hear her above the noise. He smiled and then closed his eyes dropping his hand from her grasp.
"Hurry, God dam it," the paramedic shouted as he banged on the ambulance wall to the driver. Colin opened his eyes once more and looked at Belinda. Panic overflowed her as she looked at his face and saw that the whites of his eyes were turning red and little droplets of blood were seeping down his cheeks like tears.
"Colin, don't you leave me," she yelled almost hysterically as they pulled up into the emergency department. As soon as they got him out of the ambulance, the doctors rushed him away and almost immediately a nurse came over to Belinda, putting her arm around her and ushering her into a waiting room that had some coffee waiting on a table in one corner.

The nurse poured Belinda a cup and placed it into her hand before leaving, giving the excuse of finding out what was happening. After a while and with the cool coffee still clutched in her hands, not even a sip being taken, Belinda stood up and walked over to the window. It was quite late in the evening and the sun had almost set sending shimmering colours of red throughout the sky. What seemed like a lifetime passed before a doctor walked in with a nurse in tow before closing the door behind him. By the look on the doctor's face, Belinda knew what he was going to say and as the doctor spoke those formidable words, Belinda dropped her cup onto the floor weeping, right before blackness engulfed her.

      She came too laid on a couch and lifted herself up to a sitting position, which caused a painful sensation to shoot through her head and raising her hand to her temple, she focused on her surroundings. She saw that a nurse was sat in the chair next to her and on seeing Belinda wake up, came over and rested her hand on her arm. For a few seconds Belinda wondered where she was, then the last memory of the doctor talking to her flooded back into her mind, terrible, horrifying memories which made Belinda cry out in pain, as if a knife had stabbed her right in her heart and sliced it in two.
"Can I see him?" she sobbed almost at a whisper, not sure if she could actually go through with it or not.
"Of course, I'll just go and see the doctor." With this, the nurse left Belinda alone in the waiting room; her mind went blank as if every thought had been wiped away, causing Belinda to shake her head to try to clear herself into thinking straight. The nurse came back into the room and escorted her to where Colin was, to where they had been working on her beloved husband. The nurse stayed with her as she walked over to his side and as she looked down at his face, she felt nothing, no sorrow and no love, it was as if her feelings and emotions had been switched off.
"He looks like he's asleep......... can I have a minute alone," she asked the nurse who just nodded and left the room. For a couple of minutes she couldn't think of anything. She knew her heart had turned itself off and that there were no emotions to be let out. What was wrong with her and why couldn't she see the situation for what it really was. All of a sudden, she had to gasp for air as a rush of heat raced up her body and when it reached her heart and then her head, anger followed swelling up through her body, making her tremble as she saw red.
"WHY DID YOU LEAVE ME?" she screamed at Colin as she buried her head in his chest, sobs wrenching from her throat. Feeling her body shaking as she released the tears that had built up, she lifted her head and placed a kiss on his lips. She glided her fingers down his cheek feeling the softness that she had known for the last year or so, knowing that this would be the last time.

"I'm sorry I shouted at you, it's just that we had only just got together and we had a whole life ahead of us. I wish you hadn't left me." Belinda laid her head once more against his chest.
"I didn't even get the chance to say goodbye," she sobbed the last sentence out as the nurse came back in and put her arm around Belinda's shoulder.
"Let it out honey, let it all out."

The next few days went in a blur with everyone coming and going from her apartment. Funny how it had been their apartment just 5 days ago. Later on that afternoon she would be attending a ceremony with many of their friends to lay Colin to rest forever. As one of her friends came and sat down next to her, Belinda cried once again as she hadn't been able to stop for more than a few minutes at a time since it happened.
"Why did it have to happen to him Jane, he was only 29 years old." Belinda's heart gave a jolt of pain, which caused her to take a gulp of air to steady herself.
"I don't know why it happened Belinda and I don't really know what to say to you to help you." Her friend smiled and put an arm around her shoulder, bringing her to rest against her for comfort. Later on that night, after everyone had left after given their condolences and had said how lovely the funeral had been, Belinda walked into the bedroom and looked around. The tears started to pour once again as she saw that the bed was still unmade from the last night that they had shared together and she could still smell the scent of their lovemaking in the air. This had been the first time she had dared go in there since .... she couldn't even say that word, maybe in time, but not yet. She hadn't even stayed at the apartment since it happened, never mind go into their bedroom. Turning around and leaving the room, she closed the door and took a blanket from the airing cupboard to throw on the couch. This would have to do for now until she felt brave enough to tackle going into the bedroom once again and she knew that it could be quite a while before that would happen. Throwing herself on the couch, the room that had witnessed so much laughter and happiness was now witnessing sadness, as it filled with the sounds of mourning and sorrow.

Chapter One

One year later

John arrived at work packed with paperwork in his briefcase also lugging a handful of plans with him. He hoped to complete a client's drawings for his new building by the end of the week. He had decided long ago that God didn't put enough hours into one day for everything to be completed. He walked into the foyer of the office building, and greeted the staff, before walking into his office. Whom should he see but his best friend Peter sat in his chair with his feet upon the desk. Peter did have his own office, although he hardly ever seemed to be in it.
"Hi mate," he said grinning but not getting up. Seeing all the work that John was toting round with him, he pulled a face, "You planning to do some work then today," he said sarcastically but smiling at the same time. Then deciding he'd better get up and help his friend before he dropped the plans all over the floor, he rose from his seat and grabbed them out from under his arm and placed them on John's desk. John put down his briefcase by the side of his desk before reaching for the intercom and pressing a button to speak to his secretary.
"Helen, be a darling and bring me a strong coffee please."
"Of course, I won't be a moment," came the reply, and John slumped down in his seat at his desk and smirked at Peter.
"What do you want this early in a morning Peter? You're not usually in yet, even at this time." Glancing down at his watch, he saw it wasn't even 8.30 am yet, he knew Peter never rolled in until at least 9 am. He smiled at Peter,
"What is it, come on, spit it out." Peter leaned the back of his long legs against the desk and grimaced at his friend.
"Can't I even come in here on this lovely, fine morning, and greet a friend with a simple good morning."
"Yeah, right, you never do anything without a reason," laughed John. At that moment, Helen came in holding two cups of coffee in her hands.
"I have never known you to deny yourself some extra caffeine Peter," she was smiling as she came in and smiling as she walked out.
"I think," said John "If you weren't married, you'd stand a chance there mate." looking towards the door that Helen had just exited from.
"Don't be daft pal," replied Peter, "she smiles at all the men." They both laughed knowing full well that Helen was on the lookout for a husband, she was a lovely girl, they both knew that, she was also a very active and enthusiastic athlete. The man who was to marry her would have to be an Olympic athlete to keep up with her stamina. Both John and Peter were just after a quiet life, no extra activities involved, well not too much anyway, except for the imperative marital activity that was essential for the human race to survive, and that was definitely an activity that didn't need thinking about twice before partaking on.

Although John had no intentions of ever marrying, so that type of activity with someone permanent was definitely out of the question for him.

"What is it that you really want then?" asked John, because he really did know his friend quite well and knew there was something on his mind.

"Well, Sharon and I are going out tonight, to that restaurant that we all went to last weekend, the 'Sunrise to Sunset'. Do you remember?" Not waiting for John to answer he carried on, "anyway her cousin is up visiting, we thought......" John immediately interrupted, as he knew where this was heading.

"Oh no, I'm not being dragged into a blind date, forget it." Waving his hands at either side of himself.

"Oh come on mate, do this for me, for Sharon." Peter looked at John with the bottom of his lip sticking out.

"There's no point in pouting pal, that don't work with me. You may be able to work your way around Sharon with that look, but it don't do nothing for me." John said as he opened his briefcase and took out some of his files. Opening them up and placing them on his desk, he looked up to see Peter still looking at him with that pouted lip.

"Get out of her mate, before the wind changes and you get stuck like that." Peter stood up, sighed and walked over to door opening it to leave.

"See you at 7.30pm then." he said with a smirk on his face, closing the door on John's protests. It wasn't that John had any objections to going on a blind date, but the fact of the matter was that he wasn't ready for a new relationship yet, his last one had been disastrous. He didn't want any woman getting the wrong impression by agreeing to go out with them. He would go tonight, he knew that, but only for Sharon's sake. He took pity on her for having to put up with someone like Peter, as he had told her often enough to the sounds of Peter grumbling. They all knew it was in fun and that was why he would oblige to this 'blind date'. As long as he made it quite clear from the start that this was just a friendly outing with a few friends, then there shouldn't be any problem.

Looking in the mirror at his reflection before he left his apartment, he realised that he wasn't getting any younger, but women scared him somewhat. He had earned quite a substantial amount of money over the last few years and found that most of the women he had seen had wanted to go out with him because of this, to see what they could get from him. 'How do you know when they're being truthful, there's no way you can tell if someone's lying to you, that's the hard thing. Being able to trust someone again whole heartedly, without question'. John realised that he was talking to himself again, it was becoming quite a habit of late. Laughing at himself he closed the door to his apartment and went down the few steps into the street below and got into his car, a black Porsche. One of the luxuries he had let himself indulge in recently, at least a car can't do the dirty on you.

Whilst driving to the restaurant where he was to meet Peter, Sharon and the beautiful cousin, or so he had been told, he thought back to the last time Peter had sucked him into going on a blind date with him. What a disaster that had been, the woman was dressed in clothes that made her look a 'Lady of the night' and what the barman had said to John had him heading for the exit quick smart.

"I see you've been down town John," looking over at his date and winking. Peter said John's face was a picture, he had never been so embarrassed in all his life. But he was sure that Sharon's cousin couldn't in no way be anything as bad as that, after all she was family, but still the situation managed to create a moan out of him. Shaking his head and sighing, he arrived at the restaurant with a few minutes to spare, sitting in the car, he leaned his head back against the headrest and closed his eyes. He must have gently nodded off because the next thing he knew, there was a knock on the windscreen and he saw Peter smiling in through the glass. John got out of the car and slammed it shut.

"You can't be bored already mate, you haven't even met her yet," laughed his friend, slapping him on the back as they both walked into the restaurant. Sharon introduced her cousin as Cheryl and John nodded to her, shaking her hand and being very thankful that she was dressed quite appropriately and was charmingly attractive.

The evening went without any pitfalls and John found that Cheryl was indeed a lovely woman, very elegant and by all means pleasing to the eye, but there was that certain something that was missing. Maybe his mind was blocking any kind of attraction, not giving anything a chance to start but John was a perfect gentleman though and filled her glass, gave polite conversation and even danced with her. When it was time for them to say their goodbyes, John courteously took Cheryl back to Peter and Sharon's house.

"I enjoyed this evening, thank you," he said trying to sound grateful but then again, not to sound eager for a repeat performance.

"Thank you," she replied, "I had a lovely time too, I'm glad that Sharon talked me into going out this evening. I miss my fiancée terribly and I'm looking forward to him coming home." John looked over at the window where Peter was peeking out through the curtains. He could see his shoulders moving up and down, no doubt roaring with laughter. I'll kill him, he thought. Wait until I see him tomorrow, he did this on purpose. Smiling at Cheryl, he kissed her politely on her cheek and bid her farewell. When he got back to his apartment the phone was ringing.

"Hello," He answered.

"Sorry about that mate, I couldn't help it," said Peter in-between sniggering. "Cheryl needed a good night out and she agreed to play the role, not letting you know that she was engaged. She didn't like it at first, didn't like the idea of leading you on, but when I had told her that you weren't interested in dating anyone at the moment, she relented and thought it would be fun."

John did see the funny side of it and they both were laughing before the end of the conversation.

"Goodnight Peter." He said and hung up. 'I'm still going to kill him, one of these days', he said to himself whilst yawning. He went into the bedroom to change, laid on the bed and got his book from the bedside cabinet to read for a little while. He found reading relaxed him, his mind was usually too wound up to sleep, and reading a couple of chapters always sedated his brain. Within minutes he was asleep with the book open at the page where he had left it.

Chapter Two

Belinda walked around her small London apartment, clasping her hands together nervously, feeling her body trembling as she tried to fight back the tears that threatened to overflow. She knew she was on her own now and had been for the past year, she'd found it extremely hard most of the time, the last 12 months hadn't been easy and existence had been more like a dream. Just living the days by going through the motions, everything in a sort of haze, in some ways not feeling quite real enough to care about what she did with her life. Today, she had been unable to keep her barrier up any longer, just 12 months since the horrific event that had shattered her life, making this the first anniversary since Colin, her dearest beloved, had collapsed and died from a brain haemorrhage. One moment she had been with her husband, talking to him, jesting, joking with him, crying and loving him and the next, he was gone leaving her alone, stunned and in total shock.

The weekend before death had entered their home and snatched her love away, they had made inundated love, as they often did most nights. But this particular time had been extra special. Colin had taken her away for a romantic and unadulterated weekend to celebrate his promotion at work. They had gone back to a little beach house on the West Coast of Wales that they had rented for their honeymoon. It was in a little town called Hope, hope being a word that they had used a lot in their diminutive time that they had had together. Hope for a future of happiness and even children. The beach house had been strikingly impressive with ivy running up along both sides of the building, with little white buds scattered here and there ready to open and bring beauty into the world. At the front, there were different coloured roses climbing up over the door and along some trestles that had been built to stretch over the front onto the porch. The view from the bedroom was of the sea and at night they could hear the lapping of the waves against the shore, bringing a pleasant sense of peace and calm into their little room. And the gulls sometimes landed on their little love nest, their claws making little pit-a-pat noises as they walked, awaking them out of slumber and into the arms of loving wonder.

They had spent the first night making love on a secluded part of the beach. Colin had laid a blanket between two sand dunes and these mounds acted as their only protection from the slight cool breezes of Spring. They were totally secluded, in a make believe world of their own, with only the gulls to witness the passion that was evident for each other. The evening before coming home, they had gone into town and dined at an exclusive restaurant, both drinking Champagne to celebrate life. They had only been married for 2 years, but Belinda looked upon those brief but ecstatic few years as an exhilarating time.

Thinking back before that grievous and tragic catastrophe that had thrown her emotions into utter turmoil, they had both expected to be together forever. Colin had proposed to her after only 6 months of seeing her and winning her heart, the love for each other being very apparent from the first day. It had been the happiest time of her life when she had walked down the aisle with her father at her side, uniting herself with the man she had loved and still did love, Colin was eagerly waiting for her to stand by him in front of the priest. She remembered that she'd had tears in her eyes as he had promised to love her until 'death do us part………' little did she realise that death would part them so quickly, their life together had only just started, and it was distressing being wrenched away from each other so suddenly.

At the beginning of their marriage and even before, they had both discussed that concentrating on their careers for a little while was for the best before starting a family. Colin had said that eventually he would want a family, maybe even as large as a football team. Walking around the kitchen, she remembered how she had gasped and sniggered at Colin with the thought of so many children in the house. She had warned him that their love life would go down the tube after chasing that many children around the home all day. He had been very quick to clear his throat and change his mind to just 2 or 3. Now Belinda's only regret, a remorse that was deep rooted in her heart, was that they'd hadn't had a child, someone to remind her of him whenever she was feeling lonely, to cuddle and feel him near. She wanted to look into their child's face and see something of Colin looking back. She wished that she'd had something to prove that their love had existed and would still carry on. Everyone would've been able to say, 'look there's Belinda's and Colin's little one, isn't he growing and doesn't he look just like his dad.' But that's obviously not what everyone was saying. She picked up her cup of coffee and took a sip, contorting her face, acknowledging that she had left it on the counter too long and it was now stone cold. Throwing it into the sink, she recalled the words of her friends and family.
"Time for you to move on Belinda." She really wanted to, but it was so hard. If she could just get through today, then maybe she could get through anything. She had been feeling stronger at each passing day, the smile that had been lost for a while lifted its head sometimes, and she had noticed a bounce in her step now and again. But today, had thrown her a little, after all this had been the big day, when the grim reaper had touched her love on his shoulder, and took him away.

Getting on with her life was the main reason why she'd decided to move away and quit her job as a Secretary and start writing short stories, it wasn't a light decision, as she had been contemplating it for a few months now.

She had at the beginning felt uneasy about her decision, telling herself that she wasn't doing this to forget Colin, but so much of her old life reminded her of him, everywhere she went, everywhere she looked, the corner shop, the local pub and even the local fish & chip shop where they would go every Monday night etc. Sometimes it was the little things that hurt the most, one day, she had found one of his shirts in her dresser, she had spent the next couple of hours crying on the bed whilst clinging to the garment, rocking back and forth, lulling herself to sleep. Colin's energy was all around, which was hardly surprising since they had shared their life together in every aspect imaginable. She still loved Colin, she always would, but that love had to be put aside now. Colin had come into her life at a time when she was in despair of ever loving again. She'd had an extremely bad relationship with a man before who had been violent towards her, physically and mentally. Colin had been the one to open up her heart and teach her the true meaning of love and trust again. She would never stop thinking about him and she would never stop loving him as he had been an important part of her life, but she knew she had to move forward on her own now.

Grabbing her keys, she left the apartment and drove out of the city along the motorway towards Colin's home village which luckily wasn't too far away. Once there, she stopped and parked in the local supermarket car park. The florist shop was only 2 minutes' walk so it didn't take long before she was setting off again with a bouquet of flowers beside her on the passenger seat. Arriving at the cemetery, she parked the car and got out, noting that the sky was quite cloudy but the sun still managed to peak its head out of one of the clouds as if waving hello. Walking towards his grave, she glanced at all the other graves thinking of all the sorrow that these departed souls had left behind them. She knelt down and placed the bouquet on Colin's grave talking to him and telling him all about her plans and knowing in her heart what he would have said if he could.
"Go for it girl, you can do it." Feeling tears fall down her cheek, she wiped them away with the back of her hand and laughed.
"I love you Colin," was all she said as she stood and blew him a kiss before leaving.

That evening, as the sun was beginning to set she ambled over to the window and heard some noises from outside. Looking out, she caught a glimpse of two young people arguing at the side of a car. The view from the window wasn't anything spectacular, but both her and Colin hadn't rented the apartment for the view. It had been in both vicinities of their work and was in the right price range. Looking at the shops on the opposite side of the road, she saw the boutique that she sometimes visited when wanting something quick to wear when an occasion had been sprung on her unexpectedly.

Next to the boutique, there was the local fish and chip shop, quite a few happy hours had been spent going there for both of them. She smiled recalling one occasion when they'd had a chip fight, which ended up with Colin feeling his way around her clothes that she was still wearing with his mouth, in search of any stray chips that were hidden for him to eat. Giggling, she pulled the curtains closed. She would have to do that more often reminiscing about the good times and not contemplating on the last, abominable and painful event. Catching her breath, she recalled being at the hospital, the doctor informing her of Colin's death. The only thing that had disturbed her the most after the initial shock, was that she hadn't been able to say goodbye. Blinking back tears, she shook her head.
"Stop this now, you promised to think only of the good," she quickly scolded herself as she walked back into the kitchen, maybe a good strong coffee would help her concentrate. She'd had a really hard time focusing on anything lately, her mind seeming constantly clouded. Even late at night, when all the noises from outside had calmed down, her neighbours being home from work had stopped their arguing, screaming and slamming their doors. Her mind still tried to make sense of everything that was going on in her life, but without success and as everything was coming into her mind all at once, she felt like she was going crazy, so many innocent thoughts, guilty emotions all blending into one. When she had been on her daily walks to try and clear her mind, she had returned with more confusion cluttering her senses than when she left. There wasn't anywhere peaceful to go during the day to collect her thoughts, sometimes the noise and heat of the water of the shower relaxed her, taking her away for just a few brief minutes to another world, void of emotions that pulled and tore at her heart. It had been futile during the day for her mind to roam away to a distant place of peace, with everyone going about their daily lives, the hustle and bustle of city life on their heels and she had never gone out after dark, as it was too dangerous. It was most disturbing not being able to clear her consciousness of all its clutter and with this agitation came a diversion for her passion of life. But hopefully, with a new direction for her life to follow, a new path to go down, her stories might give some meaning to her pathetic little life, because that's all it was at the moment.

She leaned back on her chair away from the computer, giving a deep sigh whilst rubbing the bridge of her nose. 'This is absolutely hopeless, I need to get away from here.' She said aloud as she knew she shouldn't have tried to start on her stories before moving, but she was eager, although now she knew that enthusiasm had been a mistake on her part, but never mind, a lesson learned at least. Getting up and walking over to the coffee table in the living room, she picked up the newspaper that she had remembered to buy at the last minute on her way home from seeing her friends at the Sports Centre. She often went there for a workout of aerobics after work, at least twice a week. It had been a time to enjoy her friends company and unwind a little.

She went and sat on the couch to scan through the paper, and came across what she was looking for, the 'to let' advertisements, she'd had to order this newspaper specially since it was a local newspaper from up north in the Lake District. Hopefully she could find something away from the City and far into the countryside, if it was going to take drastic measures to get her life back in order and her stories completed and written, then she would take them. She got her pen out of the drawer under her T.V. and circled the advertisements that appealed to her the most. Upon completion of that task, she went into the kitchen and made herself another strong cup of coffee. Once she was away from here and she could relax more, maybe she would be able to cut down on so much caffeine that she was pouring into her system. With the coffee and the newspaper in one hand, she grabbed the telephone with the other and sat by the window. She looked at the first one she had circled. 'A single person or couple wanted to look after a two bedroom cottage in the village of Hathersage, Hope Valley in Derbyshire for the Summer/Autumn whilst owners on vacation.' This sounded perfect. She had always loved Derbyshire, it was so peaceful in some of the villages there and she was hoping this village would be one of them. She dialled the number and almost immediately someone answered. After a short but sweet conversation, she replaced the receiver back onto the telephone and sat back on the couch, tucking her feet under her.
"First time lucky hopefully." She said smiling as she took another sip of her much needed stimulant. A meeting had been arranged with the owner of the cottage for this weekend. Taking a sip of her coffee she smiled to herself, this was really satisfying, taking charge of her life at long last and it definitely felt right. Maybe she would be lucky on her first go at renting a place, she and Colin had looked at quite a few places before settling on one, but maybe her luck was changing and it would be different this time. She telephoned her good friend Craig who quickly gave her the directions on how to get to Hathersage. She knew she could rely on Craig to tell her how to get there, he knew how to get to anywhere, as he was a truck driver and his work took him all over the country, sometimes even abroad.

Belinda was absorbed deep in thought as she drove along the country lane that led to Hathersage. She glanced at the scenery and inhaled deeply, it was very impressive. It had been a long time since she had been away from the city and pressing the button to lower the window down, taking in the aroma of the blossoms that were flourishing. There was a cool breeze blowing, ever so faintly, just like a bird fluttering its wings, this extenuated the scent of the flowers, that blossomed on the trees and in the fields. She took in another deep breath and smiled, a shiver went through her body.
"This is right Colin, I can feel it," she smiled as she came to a stop outside a small off licence. Leaving her car, she walked into the store and had a look around, a typical country shop, she thought.

There were shelves with basic food items, cereal, canned foods, there was a whole section in one corner that housed magazines, papers and even a few DVD's. Going towards the fridge, she opened one of the 2 vertical doors that stood side by side and reaching in she clasped a cold can of cola. As she walked out of the shop, she could feel the warm breeze whisper through her hair and refresh her skin as she clambered back into her car to carry on with her journey of adventure.

Although summer was due to raise its head and bring warmth and serenity to the world soon, she could see the sun shining through the clouds trying to gain control over spring that was trying vengefully to hang on. The trees had luxuriated and come into full bloom and were leaning over towards the road, as if showing off their elegant beauty and they appeared to be shouting to anyone that would hear them saying 'Look at us, aren't we exquisite?' The scenery here in this part of the country was unquestionably picturesque, with the small country cottages on the sides of the road and the petite, but very quaint church, that was set back giving its surrounding a more of an arcane look, making the whole representation look like something off a picture postcard. Glancing down at the directions on the piece of paper that she had laid on the passenger seat, she knew that it wouldn't be much further now.

Pulling up at the cottage 20 minutes later, a woman whom Belinda thought to be around 50 years old came out to greet her.
"Hello my dear, I presume you are Belinda, my name is Carol." Belinda approached the woman with a handshake and followed her inside the cottage. Offering Belinda a drink, which she politely accepted she commenced to show her around. Talk about falling in love at first sight with a man, this was the feeling that overcame Belinda as she walked through the cottage, enabling her to view and take in the overall picture of the place. After Carol had looked at her references and seeming pleased with what she read, she offered Belinda the place and she didn't even have to hesitate when asked if she would like to rent it. She would be mad to pass up a place as serene and placid as this one. She had looked at a few others in the paper the previous night, but she knew that the paper could be put in the bin now, her search was over, and very quickly too. Looking at the keys a little while later, after writing Carol a queue for the first 2 months, she shook the keys listening to them rattle and then clasped them in her hands as she jumped up and down. This was it, she had done it, she had taken the first step into a new beginning and hopefully a new life, This was just what was needed for her to concentrate on her stories and to help her make new memories of a different life to come. It was a pity that she had to go back to the city to arrange the move, she did so wish she could have stayed right then and there, but within a week everything was packed and transported out to the cottage.

Luckily she found a reputable moving firm that didn't cost her an arm and a leg for their charges.

On her last night in the City, she had arranged to go out to dinner with her friends and to a nightclub afterwards. There was a quaint little restaurant about 10 miles outside of the city that she had heard about and had mentioned to her friends, so that's where they were all headed that night. One of her friends who was called Fiona had agreed to drive and didn't mind playing chaperone to everyone else as she didn't drink, so it was Fiona who had come and picked Belinda up.

Once they were all seated in their seats at their table in the restaurant, Belinda ordered her meal and whilst the rest of her friends placed their orders, she went to the Bar to get the first round of drinks. Once she was seated back with her friends and all refreshments were in the right hands, Belinda's friend Fiona nudged her and pointed over to a couple sitting a few tables away from them.
"Have you seen Mr Wonderful over there," she said grinning from ear to ear. Belinda glanced sideways to have a better look, and at the same time, the handsome stranger looked her way. Belinda felt flutters in her stomach like butterflies trying to escape and she could feel her embarrassment rush over her face. She turned her head quickly and looked at Fiona and they both burst into fits of laugher.
"Very nice," Belinda said as she took a sip of her drink, resisting the temptation to sneak another peep. It was quite like a hen party the way they all roared with merriment and made quite a commotion, embarrassing Belinda with wolf whistling at the very cute guy whom she and Fiona had looked at earlier. 'Where did he come from' thought Belinda, she herself thought he was something else and quite a pleasing eyeful. His face was handsome but strong at the same time, very strong cheekbones and his jaw was wide and stern looking, but exquisite. His hair was dark brown, cut like Tom Cruise did in Top Gun, except for the whispers of grey disclosing just above his ears. She couldn't tell the colour of his eyes but she guessed they were either brown or green, and when he smiled, his eyes shone also. He was definitely turning a few heads in his direction from other tables of the fairer sex.
"I don't know who he is," said Sarah, "but I wish he would look in my direction, I could blow a kiss to him." All the others laughed and made such a lot of noise, that one of the waiter's came over and asked them, very politely, to quiet down.

John looked over his companion's shoulder.
"Who are all those cackling hens, they are really making a fool of themselves." He stated although he did find one of them startlingly sexy. She had exceptional dark hair, almost sheer black and slightly wavy, which fell delicately upon her shoulders and her face was oval in shape with high cheekbones.

Her smile was very tantalising, and the lips of that smile just begged to be kissed. 'I bet her eyes are green or hazel,' he thought. Just then he realised that someone was talking to him, quickly focusing his eyes back on his date he smiled at her.

"Never mind," said Helen. "Just ignore them and they might go away." As John looked over, his eyes connected with Belinda's once again. 'Wow, she is something,' thought John. He could see that she was embarrassed, as she lowered her eyes and turned away quickly taking a sip of her drink. Looking at his date and feeling very embarrassed about thinking of another woman whilst he wined and dined another, he found himself turning slightly red as he looked down hoping Helen hadn't seen him. Helen had been his secretary for almost 3 years now and she was a very attractive woman, but they were just good friends, who now and again went out and had a meal together and at the same time enjoyed each other's company. He had thought at one time, seeing if there could be more between them and she had also been thinking about it, but when they did kiss, once, they had ended up laughing whilst their lips were pressed together. Helen stating that it was like kissing her brother. If it had been anyone else, John might have been offended, but he too felt the same. So at least they knew where they stood and that definitely had put a stop to any ideas floating about in their minds of a relationship together. They were in London at the moment attending a seminar, John being the main speaker as he was an excellent architect with quite a few years of experience behind him. It was at one of the local colleges that specialised in developing the talents of budding architects of the future. He shook his head, even so, being just friends still didn't excuse him from the deplorable behaviour that he had been displaying just now, he was going to have to concentrate on Helen more and ignore the luscious dark haired beauty a few feet away from him.

Belinda met his eyes once again and felt them run over her and even though he could only see her from the side, he must have liked what he saw, because a little smirk crept into one corner of his mouth before his attention was brought back to his date by her talking to him. Turning away, she blushed and secretly smiled. 'He was indeed extremely handsome', she thought, hoping that she hadn't actually said that out loud. She glanced over at her friends to see if there was any reaction to what she thought she might have said, but when there wasn't, she sighed and relaxed, taking another sip of her drink.

When they had finished their main meal and were waiting for the desert trolley to be brought over for them to ogle at, Belinda glanced again over to the stunningly dark, virile man whom she had taken quite a liking to, but to her disappointment, the table where he and his date had been sat was now empty. Belinda moaned and turned to her friends.
"Well, that hunk has gone, but never mind, it was nice having something so sumptuous to look at for a while."

"Well I could have definitely had him for desert any time." roared Fiona and more laugher exploded from their table and the waiter, who was waiting for their order, made a slight grunting noise as if to say, come on now ladies, calm down.

After deserts were all consumed and everyone was gratified and contented, they went outside into the cool air and all climbed back into the car. Next was the exclusive nightclub. Belinda wasn't really into discos and flashing lights, now and again she thought it was OK and had gone out with Colin a couple of times, but her friends went out every weekend, saying that you didn't know life until you hit the nightclubs at least once a week. They had tried to get her to go with them before, but Belinda preferred to stay in and read a good book, her friends used to kid her about her ageing too soon but that was just her way and she liked it. She had relented this time as it was her last night with her friends, at least until the end of the summer and she felt she couldn't let them down, she would humour them and go wherever they wanted, just for tonight anyway. When they entered the nightclub, all her friends bombarded the bar to collect their thirst quenchers, grabbing Belinda and placing a glass of wine in her hands. After walking around for a few minutes they managed to find an empty booth, all agreeing that they should sit for a while and let their meal settle before tackling the dance floor. All of a sudden Fiona screamed out loud, which luckily for her not many people could hear because of the loud music, she nearly choked on her drink whilst pointing in the direction of the bar, looking over, Belinda couldn't believe her eyes when whom should she behold but Mr Wonderful. He was ordering a drink and had settled his very taut, pinchable derrière on a bar seat. He had one arm placed on the bar and was looking around the dance floor, Belinda looked around but couldn't see his date, maybe she was in the lady's room, she thought and even though she knew he hadn't seen her, she felt a wave of heat flush through her and up her body, no doubt reddening her face.

John took his pint of lager off the barman and swivelled around in his seat. He took a sip and lazily looked around the place. Letting the drink slowly drop from his lips, his eyes connected with a group of women in a corner booth not far from the bar. His heart began to beat faster and his senses heightened as he watched Belinda for a few minutes before she and her friends took to the dance floor, some of her mates grabbing a fellow or two to dance with them. He took a sigh of relief when he observed that Belinda wasn't one of them, although what it had to do with him he didn't know, he just knew it felt good. John let his eyes wander over Belinda's slim body, watching the way her body swayed to the music and noticing how the dress she wore swished around her as she moved. His pulse quickened and his eyes dilated wider as they concentrated on the way her body curved and swayed to the rhythm of the music.

He thought about what she would be like cavorting on top of him in bed. John's quickly supped his pint and nearly choked on that thought. What made him think something like that? Placing his empty glass back onto the bar, he left the nightclub. He'd taken Helen back to the hotel first as he knew that this wasn't her scene, it wasn't his really, but he felt like listening to some heavy dance sounds before retiring to his hotel room.
Maybe then, the quietness and serenity of the place would lull him to sleep, Once got back to his hotel, he had a shower and put the TV on, maybe there was something showing that would lull him to sleep.

After a while, Belinda and her friends left the nightclub and went to the local Chinese. The girls said it was a tradition at the end of any night out, to get a curry and invade one of their homes and crash out for the few hours that was left. Luckily Belinda's apartment wasn't voted to be used this time, as everything was in boxes large and small and the apartment looked more like a storage place than a home, all ready for tomorrow's move. Once at Deborah's house, they all changed into their night attire and cluttered up the living room with their Chinese food and glasses of wine. "Boy, wasn't that man at the restaurant and the nightclub a hunk or what?" said one of her friends, making the rest of them scream like teenagers.
"I'd jump his bones any day," said Fiona. "We should've brought him home and drawn straws to see who had him first." Howling with laugher, Belinda thought back to when their eyes had connected in the restaurant. Not recognising herself as the one speaking, gasped at what she heard herself say next.
"Bag's I would have got him first, as I'm the one that's leaving tomorrow." she had said pointing her nose in the air whilst holding her glass up, creating more howls of laughter and a couple of screams. Fiona stood up and lifted her glass in her hand as she pointed it to Belinda.
"To Belinda, for finally coming out of her shell and seeing at last what a mere male can do for a woman's libido." Everyone raised their glasses and toasted her, laughing hysterically afterwards.

In the morning, as they went their separate ways, they all said their goodbyes and promised each other that they would write. They had been really good friends to her and had helped her through this last year like troopers and she would miss them terribly for the next few months.

Chapter Three

There was Belinda, standing under the waterfall letting the cool refreshing water run over her body. The waterfall was against a high hill, nearly closed in by the trees and bushes that lined the river which ran from the hill. He was stood on a path at the side of the river about 30 feet from the waterfall. There were many green plants lining the banks at both sides and flush greenery occupied the river itself. He could hear birds singing and saw that the river was alive with its own type of life, scurrying and hovering over the Lilly pads Little bubbles escaped from below the water and broke free, making tiny popping noises now and again. He looked over at the waterfall to take another look at this raving goddess who was stood before him making the decision to saunter a little further up the path towards her, hoping that she wouldn't notice him. He felt like a peeping tom watching her like this, but she enthralled him and the way she moved her body under the water had an exhilarating effect on him. His heartbeat accelerated, making him aware that his blood was pumping faster around his body and as the sun shone on her, it caused the droplets of water to gleam and illuminate the pale complexion of her skin reminding him of a porcelain doll. She swept her hands up and down her body soaking the water into her clothes, which made them cling and slide around her skin and as he looked up to her face, he could tell she was in a world of her own, totally unaware of anyone else observing her movements. She was smiling, no doubt she liked the freshness of the water cooling her skin and how he wished that he was doing that. If she was tormenting a man now without even realising it, what could she do when she was aware of the power that she had? The inkling of that thought was electrifying. God knows what she would do if she knew that he was watching her. Would she scream, run or would she keep on smiling, becoming a tease? All sorts of theories set forth spinning through his mind.

As she ran her hands through her hair, she raised her head up towards the sun and closed her eyes. A wave of energy ran down through his body, making him shudder. God she was beautiful. Her dark, sparkling hair hung down onto her shoulders clinging to her clothes and the bare skin on the back of her neck, with the light of the sun shining on it, her hair glistened a blazing tinge of Blue. The sun's rays were very warm today, or was it the fire within his own body heating up from desire of wanting this seductress who stood before him. If it weren't for the worry of frightening her, he would have urged himself over and joined her under there. Not just to feel the coolness of the water, but to feel her near him and to be able to see up close the reaction of what this water was doing to her. The way her mouth opened and curled as she ran her hands over herself, it was obvious that she was enjoying herself, letting the water run down her body.

He envied the cool drops of liquid and wished that he could cover her like the water was doing, touching every part of her as it ran down her body onto the ground. His body reacted like it was going into spasm just thinking about it, he hadn't even talked to her in years and yet, here again he was smitten. His manhood was arousing with stimulating thoughts of desire and passion, how he wanted to be able to caress her to the point of fulfilment. John locked his eyes shut and shook his head, grimacing at what he was thinking, he never thought like that and not especially about a woman he didn't even know, how could he do what his body was currently demanding? All reason seemed to have been obliterated from his mind. Taking a deep breath he opened his eyes, laying eyes on her once again, but this time, feeling more relaxed at getting his emotions sorted out in his head. Besides, he wasn't the sort of man to go in for things like that. He didn't agree with one-night stands because his heart had to feel something as well as his body. Even though he knew in his heart that that was the sort of person he was, his body was telling him something totally different.
'I've haven't even spoken to her,' thought John. 'What would she think, if you knew I was spying on her?'

John stood for what seemed a long time watching her and wanting so much to speak. What if she looked over and saw him gazing at her, would she think of him as some kind of pervert? Maybe he should go over to her before that happened, but what would he say? 'Hello, I think you are the most beautiful woman I have ever seen, can I join you under there and make mad, passionate love to you?' John laughed, this was absurd. She'd probably slap him in the face. He could feel the colour rising up through his body to his face, knowing how embarrassed and ashamed he would be. Looking around making sure he was alone, he straightened himself up and took a deep breath. I'll do it, I'll go over to her and somehow stay in one piece, try and not make a fool of myself and speak to her.

Belinda loved it under the waterfall. It had been a hot day, and the water was cooling her burning body from the heat of the blazing sun. She turned her head to look over at the trees that were alongside the waterfall. She knew he was standing there because she had sensed him. He had stood there before watching her, but the last time he had only stayed for a few minutes and then he was gone. Would he stay longer this time she wondered? He definitely intrigued her. She knew she had just seen him recently when she had gone out with her friends before leaving the big city. Why was he here though, in the middle of nowhere and why was he watching her with such intensity? She felt a shiver ripple through her body but it wasn't the cold water making her react like that, she knew that she was attracted to this man. There seemed to be a glow around him making his aura illuminate different colours of gold, red and orange, emanating from where, she didn't know..

Suddenly, she turned to face John and looked right at him and smiled. John gasped and felt his heart jump up into his mouth and he had to take a step back as the blood rushed up him like a tidal wave, threatening to bring him to his knees. She knew that he had seen her looking at him. He was extremely handsome and very sexy so what now? Should she go up or stay where she was. What was he thinking? She smiled and moved out of the waterfall.

'Oh my God, she's walking this way towards me,' he said quietly to himself. He could feel the blood rush up along his body once again and his legs nearly collapsed under him, as a wave of energy pulsated through him making him experience light-headedness. 'What power does this woman have over me? She's only walking up to me and I've already lost control, just imagine what would happen if she touched me. I would probably explode and another headline would appear in the next day's newspaper.' "Man found in woods, another unsolved case of human combustion." Her clothes, wet with the water clinging like leaches to her body, accentuating every move she made and even though she wasn't very near yet, he could make out the curvaceous outline of her form. What womanly contours she had, definitely very feminine and the way her hips swung from side to side when she walked, as lascivious as a woman could get. Was she teasing him or was that just the way she walked he wondered. No woman could walk like that naturally, it was in a way unnatural.

She strolled up to him very gracefully, wrapping her arms around him as he looked directly into her eyes seeing that they were a mixture of tantalising blue and green like the sea looked on a clear summer's day. She returned his gaze, penetrating into his very being and soul, making him wish there'd been something to hold onto, as his legs felt like they were going to buckle under him. Her skin was of a pale complexion, almost like milk and he could see was totally unblemished from the world's pollutions. He leaned into her body to give himself completely and it felt like he had melted right into her, becoming one mind and one body, becoming the essence of one. They didn't speak, all the time looking into each other's eyes and the smile on her lips was breath-taking. She felt his arms go around her pulling their bodies even tighter together with their lips only inches apart. He brought his hands around to cup her face. God, he was behaving like an uncontrollable school kid who couldn't restrain his hormonal hunger yet, but he couldn't help it as he had to kiss her. Gently he lowered his face to hers and as their lips met they both felt an explosion rippling through their bodies, igniting like a furnace overloaded with fuel, making their bodies and minds ache for each other. They began searching every part of each other's mouth, using their tongues to caress and explore their inner most secrets. John wanted to talk to her and to hear her voice, to say anything, just to hear her once more.

He moved his mouth gently away from hers and opened his eyes, trying to look deep into hers, but she was oblivious to the fact that he was seeking a reason for all of this as she had rested her head against his chest. He placed his hand on the back of her head and held her there, his breathing calming slightly and less ragged.

It was evident that there was a strong connection between them, she wondered if he felt the same..... he had to, he just had to. Looking up at him she smiled the most amazing smile and she felt an overwhelming desire to touch and caress his face with her hand. She drew her hand up and stroked down his cheek, hoping he didn't feel it quivering, she felt how smooth his cheek was, obviously a man of good grooming it seemed. John quickly grasped her hand and raised it up to his mouth, slowly brushing over her fingers with his lips. He looked into her eyes and then let go of her hand as he wrapped his arms around her, pulling her close before kissing her forehead. As he placed his hands on the lower part of her back, he could feel they were shivering and trembling, almost tingling at the mere touch of her. And even though her clothes were cold with the wet, he could feel the heat radiate from her body, seeping through, warm and enticing. He wondered if she could feel the heat from his body, because his temperature was definitely rising.
"Hello" said John, unsure of what to say to her, although he felt as though he knew everything there was to know about her, right now, right here, but was that possible? No, of course not. She couldn't talk as her voice had evaded her and all words seemed to have escaped from her mouth. Was this the impact that he was having on her body to strike her dumb? She raised her head and kissed John gently on the lips, not being able to reply to him with the words that he wanted to hear.

All she did was smile and John's heart melted. He moved his head closer as he returned her kisses, slowly and gently, applying more pressure with each kiss and each one increasing with passion, as they held on to each other, soaking up the heat not just from the sun, but from their bodies that craved the passionate heating rising within, someone passing by would at a glance only see one person. All of a sudden, John disappeared before her eyes, he was gone. She looked with a puzzled look on her face, wondering where he was, where she was? Why wasn't she back home at the cottage? She felt so confused and her head had started to hurt. Placing her fingers to her forehead, she tried to make sense out of what was happening. Was she dreaming? She couldn't tell. But if she wasn't, where was she?

Chapter Four

John sat bolt right up in his bed. This dream had been much more intense than last time as they had actually held and kissed each other. The mental images of the dream had been so real and not like any other dream he had ever had. John lay back on his bed, perspiration running down his face with the memory of their embrace and his body still shook with the undeniable feelings of sexual desire and emotional wanting. Just because he had seen her lately, at the restaurant and then at the nightclub, was he still so connected with her that he had now took to having erotic dreams about her? John looked towards the window and even though the curtains in his apartment were closed, he could see the rays of the morning sun shining through the gaps at the sides. He felt fatigued, this wasn't right! He should have felt good with such an erotic dream as that, but the truth of the matter was that he was exhausted, as being with her in his dream had tired his whole body and mind. His emotions started to run wild now that he was thinking of her again, remembering her under the waterfall and how she wrapped her arms around him, feeling her breasts pressing against his chest. The heat emanating from her skin and her 'come to bed' eyes gazing up at him. He shuddered and glanced down at his arousal that was beginning to stir, moaning, he realised that he'd better go and take a cold shower to cool himself off a little. The effects of his dream were evidently still with him or so it seemed, but this was madness, how could his body and mind be so moved by a woman whom he had only dreamed about, but yet the craving was so strong that it brought out his primeval instincts, not just wanting to take her and make love to her, but also to protect, love and cherish her forever. Was he that lonely in life that he had to conjure up a woman to take away his loneliness? No, of course not, his life at the moment was full of his work, his mates and it wasn't as if he had been celibate, he'd had a couple of female companions over the years, but had inevitably gone their separate ways and he always managed to find someone willing to go out with him when he was in need of a woman's company. He never did take them on the first date though, he was a man with old fashioned views and believed that some romance should be involved. He didn't want to settle down with anyone at the moment anyway, so a need for a woman like the need she made him feel, wasn't even in the equation of his life, or so he had thought. Could anyone have their mind changed so dramatically by just a couple of dreams, was that possible? Well, he guessed it was, because that is what had happened to him.

John pulled the covers back and got out of bed, he walked over to the bathroom taking his robe from the bottom of the bed as he passed. Turning on the water he made sure it was more on the cool side than warm and then looked at his reflection in the mirror.

His eyes were slightly puffy and dark, he'd have to make sure that he got some sleep tonight as he couldn't afford for these dreams to tire him so. They might affect his performance at work and he couldn't allow that to happen. He needed the commission from his clients to keep him going, he wasn't short of money by no means, but he wanted to make sure that his income was steady, and he wanted his reputation kept immaculate and refined.

As he stepped into the shower and felt the cool water run over his body. It felt exhilarating, but yet with this came back the memory Belinda in his dream, standing under the waterfall. He was now doing exactly what she had been doing, except that he was naked. blimey, that made matters worse. He could visualise her and the wetness accentuating every curve of her body as she had moved towards him, her wet clothes clinging to her curvaceous body. All the emotions and intense desires that he'd had, came rushing back with a vengeance and as John looked down he winced, so much for the cold shower, it was supposed to suppress these emotions not increase them. He stepped out of the shower, dressed and went into the kitchen to get something to eat before going to work.

He'd had a particularly eventful period of time at work considering that he was tired, but he tried not to let the lads or his secretary see him yawn, which he tended to do from time to time that day. So when he did see any of the staff lurking around his office, he sat straighter and put on his professional demeanour that was called for in his line of work, also making sure Helen brought him lots of coffee. John took pride in his work, he had worked his way up in the firm, starting off as the local run around to Vice Principal of the Company, but he still liked to get his hand in with some of the clients. He believed that you couldn't run a firm properly if you didn't keep yourself on top of what the Company was offering.

He was feeling in quite a good mood when he'd got back to the office, his new client being so impressed with the statistics of his Firm's climb into the business world, that as the meeting came to a close and they shook hands, he said that he would be bestowing on them some extra duties in the very near future. Part of his plans was to pull down one of the old abandoned cinema houses and develop it into an outstanding Theatre House.

John was glad he had gone for a drink with the lads after work before coming home, they always managed to take his mind off work and hopefully off the raving beauty, whom had taken most of his sleep and energy the night before. Whilst at the pub, Peter, his best friend had eyed him suspiciously some of the time.
"You're very quiet, John." He noted. "Everything going okay with work? Or are you lusting over Helen, quite a woman, hey."

"Yeah, mate." He had replied trying to sound nonchalant. "Just a bad night last night, really restless. Nothing to worry about and at least I didn't yawn in front of Mr Henderson, the new client. I don't think that would have gone down too well," quickly taking a sip of his drink and talking to one of the other lads, hoping that it would deter his friend from asking any more questions. Peter was a good mate and could always read into John's moods with quite a precision. He would soon realise that it wasn't just the workload that was keeping him from a good night's sleep and he didn't really want to get into any of that. He went home after promising the lads that he would play a game of darts and pool with them down at the local later on that evening. He wasn't much of a pub person, but the lads made him laugh, and he felt that he needed a lot of that lately. Walking lazily home, his thoughts went again to Belinda, he quickened his pace and was back home in no time. He hastily made himself a cup of tea and even though he wasn't very hungry, as he'd eaten a quick snack at the pub, he knew he had to eat something more substantial. Downing booze on a nearly empty stomach was a definite no. He had learned that by experience when he had been younger and naive about alcohol. He did so want to take a quick nap before going out though, so making something light had seemed the logical thing to do, maybe a salad and some boiled rice as he knew he wouldn't be able to sleep if he'd just eaten a hefty meal. He was exhausted and knew he would benefit from forty winks. The lads were expecting him to meet them at 8 pm so he knew he could sleep for at least an hour. He chuckled as he set his alarm, just to be on the safe side as he didn't want to oversleep and miss an exciting evening with the lads and he was very tired so he couldn't trust himself to wake up in time to go out. He slipped his jacket off and sat onto the bed to undo his shoelaces, pulling them off his feet he wiggled his toes that felt good, the shoes were quite new and his feet felt cramped in them, but once the leather wore some, the discomfort would go away. He loosened his tie and slipped it over his head and undid the top button of his shirt. He must have been more tired than he thought, because he was asleep before his head even touched the pillow.

    Belinda was sat in a beautiful meadow down with her head tilted and her eyes gazing up at the sky, it was a beautiful day and the sun was shining as it had done since she got there, with a cool breeze blowing the air around her. Looking around she felt nothing but confusion. How did she get here? She didn't remember walking here. There were a lot of things that were happening lately, and she didn't understand most of them either. Was she dreaming or was she losing her memory, maybe even her mind. She was just thinking about John when he appeared by her side. She was like a magnet drawing on all his strength and will power. He didn't even remember walking through the woods this time. It didn't matter if he wanted to walk away, as his legs had turned to stone and feeling so heavy that he couldn't have moved them even if he had wanted to.

Belinda was sat on the grass in a clearing not far from the waterfall and he was stood next to her. She lifted her arms and beckoned him to fall into her, to become one with her.
"Come be with me John," she whispered. Did she actually talk then or did he just sense it. He swore that her lips never moved but those thoughts were quickly lost, as he felt himself lower into her arms and when he did, it was like their bodies just moulded into one once more. Wrapping his arms around her and drawing her down onto the ground with their bodies combining together like a magnet, he didn't think that they could part even if they tried. Their bodies were quivering and sparks were flying all over the place, different colours flickering through the air creating an electrical discharge. Was he generating his own electricity? Was that what was emanating from his body and shooting through both of them, causing their heads to spin. She was the most beautiful and sensuous woman he had ever known.

"What's happening" He finally asked her, he had to before his emotions and desires got carried away, for if they did then it would be impossible for him to even speak, never mind think about what he was supposed to be saying. Belinda didn't answer, she just looked up at him and smiled, her mind whirling around and she felt dizzy once again, but elated also. He lifted up slightly off her body and closed his eyes for a moment, trying to steady his thoughts, which were racing continuously through his mind, creating all sorts of confusion. What was going on, he felt like he was going mad. He looked down into her face as she took hold of his arms and pulled him closer to her, sending another surge of energy pulsating through his body down into the pit of his stomach.
"I need to feel you against me, touching me, being close to me." She said as they entwined themselves together, binding their bodies as one so that they could feel their hearts beating and what seemed even more impossible, was that their hearts seemed to be beating the same, as one heart, with the same rhythm. God, could two people get any closer than this? Their auras were illuminating all around them, attaching themselves together and uniting them as their souls became one.

  Belinda started caressing his body, moving her hands up his back and over his shoulders, gripping his skin and making him wince with desire. He was strong and his muscles rippled under her touch surging erotic energy throughout his body. She reached up letting her fingers go through his hair, tugging at it to bring down his head to hers, filling his mouth with her kisses. His response was a deep groan that leapt from his throat as he crushed his mouth upon hers with such hunger and wanting. He needed so much to make love to her, but he knew it wouldn't be right.

With all the will power that he could muster, he pulled away from her and sat upright. Taking a deep breath he pulled his knees up and sat looking up at the sun, squinting his eyes as it shone as bright as ever. Feeling the warmth from the sun on his face was comforting and this seemed to calm some of the tension in his body. How perfect, the sun shining and a cool breeze blowing, also a beautiful woman by his side. How could this dream be so God Dam perfect? But hang on here! How did he know it was a dream? You didn't usually know when you were dreaming, something was wrong here, it had to be, but what? His heart was beating so fast that it was a wonder it didn't explode out of his chest. How in the hell were his ribs keeping it in? John's whole body was releasing male hormones that were driving her insanely crazy, the natural scent of his flesh mixed with testosterone, she could smell him, but by God, she wanted to taste him. He was so masculine more than any man that she had ever seen, muscles rippling out where she didn't even know men had them, not even Colin, God bless his soul. He was prone to eat too many chocolate éclairs, but she had loved him nevertheless. Looking at John's face whilst he gazed up at the sky, she knew that she'd seen him before, but where? They'd surely met before, hadn't they? Her head hurt, closing her eyes she looked down towards the ground as everything went black. He turned around to face her, he wanted to tell her that he loved her and that he wanted to take her in his arms, make them one and then declare his undying love to her once again. A feeling of panic rose up in him, surging through his body as he found that she was gone, looking around, she was nowhere to be seen, how could she have got away so quickly and without him noticing? He couldn't remember what transpired last time she was with him in his dream, it was all so confusing. He stood up quickly and WOW, he shouldn't have done that and stumbled as his head started to spin.

Chapter Five

John bolted upright in his bed again. 'I can't believe this is happening,' he thought trying to sort out the images racing through his mind as his heart was again beating intensely. They say that your heart only beats a certain amounts of times throughout your life, well John was sure that by the time he had reached next week his heart would have used them all up. 'Am I going crazy or what?' this idea going through his mind as he fell back onto the bed and put his hand against his forehead. 'Good God, this is absolutely insane. What the hell is happening?' He turned around and looked at the clock, 2.30 am in the morning.
"Oh no!" He had slept 8 hours straight through as not even the alarm had woken him from the impact of being with her again. John sat up on his bed and took the alarm clock from the bedside cabinet. Well it must have gone off, he thought, because it wasn't turned off. John turned the dials on the clock to check that it was working. After giving it a good shake, the alarm clock screamed at the top of its voice just letting John know that it had tried to do its duty after all, but he had only been dreaming for a few minutes anyway, surely that was all it was, it didn't seem any longer than that. Totally confused, John got up and went into the kitchen to get a drink of water, he felt positively drained and decided to go straight back to bed. He lay down but this time, no matter how hard he tried, he couldn't get back to sleep, at least not for the next couple of hours anyway, he lay there tossing and turning, his body aching for the contact of a lost loved one. He would have to think of some excuse to the lads tomorrow at work as they would think he had got some woman over and, well their imaginations would run wild. But that wouldn't be far from the truth, would it? Except that the woman in John's life wasn't real, she was only in his dreams, but it sure did feel real in his heart. The way his dreams were at the moment, he honestly couldn't tell the difference.

John didn't dream of her again that night, but the next day, there was a struggle going on between his heart and his head. No matter how much his head told his heart that she wasn't real, it still ached causing a lump in his throat. He couldn't concentrate at all on his work, so by lunchtime he went out for a walk instead of dining with his friends in the local café. Being near a small town had its advantages, there wasn't a lot of pollution as there was in the cities and if he had wanted to, he could drive in any direction and be out in the countryside within 10 minutes. Walking along the small but busy streets, he felt the breeze of the cool air refreshing him and being out in the sun, feeling its rays on his skin warming him, made him feel that he could cope with anything that life had to give, as long as he had Belinda, even if it was only in his dreams. As he looked around at all the people rushing in and out of shops and tending to their business, they all seemed to be in a world of their own and concentrating on their own lives, families and friends, these were the only things that mattered to most people, as it should be. People's families and friends should come first, business and others second, but this still gives folks the impression that mankind ignores everyone and everything around them, but everyone does that, they weren't rude people, just unaware that the world around them revolves and carries on no matter what they do or what the consequences of their actions are. He should go and sit in the park far more often than he did, listening to the birds and watching them pick up pieces of bread that someone must have left lying around or discarded, this soothed him and he found it quite refreshing. John walked back into his office and straight into the lads.

"Been out meeting your secret lady love have you?" They sniggered as they slapped John on his back.

"Got to see her sometime!" He smiled winking at Peter. They kidded him about having his lady friend over last night instead of going to see them, just like he thought they would but he didn't try to correct them, because in a way, they were right. Even John laughed with them but for totally different reasons as he knew that if he didn't laugh, he would go mad. They tried to probe him with questions. What was she like? blond or brunette, maybe a red head? But he managed to steer them away from obtaining answers and excused himself, saying he had lots of work to do

"We'll get an answer out of you tonight buddy," they said teasingly. And with that they left his office laughing together, being all macho in front of his secretary. Luckily Helen knew what fools men tend to make of themselves around women and took it all in her stride.

      That evening he went straight home and avoided the lads, as he didn't want to go to the pub at all. If they had their way, he would be down there every night; goodness knows how some of them managed to have a love life at all. They were always down at the local, telling tales of all their conquests, the thing is, they didn't realise that they were always too busy talking about their conquests to really have any. Besides he wanted to go home, his heart fluttering and beating faster just thinking about her. He was like a lovesick teenager experiencing a first love when you throw all caution to the wind and let the avalanche overtake you and cover you. John sighed. 'Listen to yourself man, rushing home to meet a woman who isn't even there.' After having a quick shower and something to eat, he turned the TV on and watched rugby. He loved watching sports, mainly football, but rugby was just as good tonight.

      Later on that evening he poured himself a beer, sat down on the couch and picked up his latest magazine of 'Computer World'. Even though he wasn't a whiz at the computer, he knew how to get around one pretty much and after looking through the articles about the latest software that was available and how it would revolutionise the world, he threw the magazine onto the coffee table and went over to the door, what he needed right now was a good walk before retiring to bed.

He grabbed his jacket on the way out and slammed the door. He'd been waiting for his neighbours to complain for a couple of days now as that darn lock was faulty and the only way to ensure that it did lock properly was to slam the door shut. Maybe tomorrow he would have a look at it as he knew how to fix them, after all, he had changed all of the locks when moving into the place, it was just a matter of taking time to go out and buy a new one and getting around to doing the dastardly deed. Walking outside, the sun was just beginning to set and this brought on a very tranquil mode to the world, he was greeted with a few hellos from neighbours as he strolled along to the park at the end of his block. He sat in one of the seats by the side watching some children playing on the swings, noticing that their parents were close by. He suddenly felt a thud by his feet and upon looking down, he saw a ball had been kicked over to him.

"Sorry mister," came a small voice, the voice of a child. John looked up and saw a little boy of about 6 or 7 looking at him with his head slightly lowered.

"No problem son," he said as he gently kicked the ball back to him. The boy picked it up and smiled a big smile as he ran off. John noticed his mother going over to the boy, putting her arms around him and talking to him and looking over at John as she did so. Probably telling him off for approaching a stranger, never mind talking to one. He could understand all the anxieties that parents had these days, the world was indeed a very troubled place to bring a child into. But that still didn't thwart his plans of one day having a wife and if the good Lord was willing, children also.

Belinda sat in the meadow; memories of when she was a child came flooding back. This was the same meadow, yes, now she was positive. Lying down, she instinctively reached for John's hand, but as she looked at her side, of course he wasn't there. Tears began falling down her cheek and as she closed her eyes, she remembered her last days in London and before she knew it, she was back there reliving this time
....

.... She was looking around at the empty apartment, all evidence of her ever being there had now been packed up and loaded into the truck. She gently closed the door and locking it before placing the key in her pocket. Those few rooms had been her home for a long time and she had to swallow as a lump came up in her throat, she felt quite sad to see it go. But then again, this was to be quite an adventure she was partaking of. If she did come back to London, she had decided already to rent a different apartment somewhere else, still on the outskirts of London like Brentwood where she had been with Colin, but in another suburb. Most of the reasons why she was moving was to lay old memories aside whilst she built new ones and she didn't want to come back and have the old memories creeping their way back into her life.

Although after a few months away, that might not take place, but she didn't want to risk it, just on the off chance of it happening.

As soon as she and the removal firm arrived at the cottage and they had unloaded all of her boxes inside, she had rooted for the coffee and kettle first and had a much deserved cuppa; she had to get her priorities right from the start she thought with a grin on her face. She connected up her computer that she had set down on a desk in front of the window in the living room, the view there was very appealing and definitely perfect for gazing out of. Looking out at the view, she now knew there was a totally new distraction facing her, how she was going to concentrate on her writing with a panoramic scene like this was hard to imagine. Her front view was like a representation of goodness and all of what the earth had to offer, but then again, a vision like this might actually give her some inspiration. As she looked out of the window, she could see a large tree in the far left-hand corner of her garden, red and orange leaves swung from every branch, a red maple tree she presumed. It was quite a large tree, very straight and grand and looking at it more closely, she could see that the branches extending over the wall, how beautiful. Over on the right was the path from the gate down to the front door, it was paved straight and neat, none of them cracked or upturned, which meant no stumbling on wobbly slabs that you sometimes get with this old type of path. The garden was mainly lawn, which was a delectable shade of green except for a small patch by the right side of the tree, where a rockery had been built, this sloped up and finally rested itself against the garden wall. She noted how the stones had been placed in strategic places and the plants had been chosen to accentuate the beauty of their colours.

On past her garden, there was a small road which was quite narrow, a lot of cars would have to go slow to pass each other, maybe even pull over onto the grass verge, depending on the size of the vehicles. Beyond the road were open fields, with splendid trees providing protection from the sun and wind for many of the animals that grazed there, and fields of different colours of green and beige were scattered across as far as the eye could see. She could imagine that the whole of the country had once looked like this, before modern day technology took over and cities were built for the more energetic lifestyle that a lot of people craved for. Over the next few days in-between unpacking, she took herself out on treks through the small village and met some of her neighbours. Luckily no one asked much about her private life, and that was what she had wanted, this time at the moment was for herself and no one else. She wasn't an ignorant person, always saying a polite hello when approached by someone and smiling was always something that she did automatically when greeting anyone. She had heard many stories of people arriving in a small community, going about their own business and by the time they left, the community knew more about them than they did themselves.

Sometimes their lives had actually been exaggerated to the point of them having had an adventure totally unbeknown to them. She was definitely an outside person and had always loved walking. She found it quite refreshing and decided that whilst she was there, she would toddle around quite often, promising herself to out into the fresh air at least once a day, no matter if it was only for 5 minutes.

Belinda had only been in the cottage for a week when she thought that if she could have a wish come true, then it would be to stay here permanently. This place was indeed heaven. Sitting out in the back garden on a deck chair that she had found in one of the sheds, she smiled once again. She had been doing that a lot lately and at one time, she had thought that her mouth had forgotten the meaning of a beam. She had never felt such oneness with a place before, so content in the milieu of this place. But it wasn't just the cottage, it was her surroundings, she felt like she belonged there and as strange as it might seem, her heart felt like it had come home, but never mind, just for the next 6 months was good enough for now, and if after then she still felt the same, then she would try and find somewhere else around here to rent on a more permanent basis, hell she might even buy somewhere and finally take root. Belinda pushed all thoughts of permanency to the back of her mind. At the moment her stories are what she came here for, well one of the reasons anyway and she now hoped she could concentrate on her first story, considering that the surroundings she was in was more serene than where she had been just last week.

Looking around the back garden, she saw that it was partly paved near the house and used mainly as a patio. A barbecue had been built onto the edge at the right-hand side and by the black markings on the metal bars, had been used quite often, evident of many a good time being had here. She could envisage all of Carol's family enjoying each other's company whilst taking in the aroma of the meat that was cooking on the grill and the view beyond their little home. Past the patio was quite a large, grand well-kept lawn with a pond in one corner. Funny how she hadn't noticed it there before. Walking over to it, she noticed some fish swimming around and observed some Lilly pads bobbing on the top, she would have a look in the cupboards in the kitchen and see if there was some fish food, it not she would go and buy some. Although she thought Carol would have said something to her, but never mind, they looked healthy enough and glad that no harm had befallen them. The water pump was making a quiet whirling sound as it created small bubbles that floated up to surface, and she watched as the fish swam in and out of them. That made her think of the shower, a lot of her friends loved their baths more, but she was a shower person.

There was nothing more refreshing than standing under a shower and letting the water beat its little pelts of droplets upon your skin to make you feel alive, especially after a day in the city, breathing in all those fumes, as they lingered on your clothes and body.

Looking up at the sky, she saw it was extraordinary, a veracious blue with miniature clouds the colour of milk dotted around. There she was smiling again, 'wonders never cease,' she thought as she walked back to the patio and sat down reaching for her drink.
"This is it," she said to herself, "here is where it all begins, I can feel it." She lifted her glass into the air. "To the future", she said as she brought the glass to her lips and tasted as the cool refreshing drink slid down her throat. Placing the drink back onto the patio table, she leaned back against the chair and closed her eyes.

Sometime later, she awoke with a shudder and although the sun was still shining she did feel a little cold. Looking at her watch, she swore quietly to herself and went back inside, stretching first to get some of the aches out of her back from being slouched for the past 2 hours and sat down at her computer with her diaries at her side and started to work. She cursed to herself under her breath, as she knew she had wasted valuable time. She had set herself a certain amount of hours to work every day, and now she had just lost 2 of them. 'Never mind', she thought, she'd make it up later. After a while, she looked away from the screen and glanced outside chuckling, the peace was unbelievable, there hadn't been any distractions at all, unless you counted the songs of the birds that could be heard outside and now and again a car would pass, but otherwise it was totally serene. She scrunched up her face but with a smile edging her lips, recognising the fact that maybe it was too quiet, what if she couldn't sleep? She was so used to the city noises from dawn to dusk, but shrugging her shoulders, she decided that she didn't really care that much and she could always put her radio on to lull her into slumber.

As the sun was setting, she sat down on the couch with a microwave meal on her lap and looked at her first attempts that she had written. Her characters assumed different names and the events happened in different places than originally, but still the outcomes had remained the same and nothing essential had been lost. None of the experiences that the main character in the story had to endure to reach the inevitable outcome had been compromised. Feelings of elation enveloped her as she was feeling very gratified with herself at the results of her first attempt, very satisfied indeed. And she knew also that Colin would have been proud of her, going out on her own and trying something totally new, although she had wanted to do this when she and Colin were married, they had both needed an income coming in.

Colin would have given her the world if he could, she knew that but they were both realistic and renting an apartment in the big city and doing the amount of socialising that London called for had needed two wages. She wasn't into clubbing and such but Colin loved mixing with others and she usually tagged along too, mainly to please him, after all she was his wife and she had loved him, she still did. She quickly finished her meal and placed the tray on the coffee table in front of her before getting up. She went over to the computer and sat back down, loading her work onto the screen. Re-reading the section that she had done earlier, she knew that she may have to alter a few words and phrases here and there, but she still felt comfortable with the results so far. This project may take longer than what she thought, but that was OK too, maybe some things you just couldn't rush. If she had to, she would call her agent and ask for an extension, but hopefully it wouldn't come to that, besides it was still early days yet.

She hadn't done much of anything socially since Colin had died, or mentally come to think of it, her mind being blank most of the time. So she'd been able to save a little money from the past year to be able to take time off like this, to close herself off from the world for at least a little while and not care what happened on the outside. She leaned back against her chair, with a confused look on her face. Had that been why she had come here, to retreat into herself and bury her head from the world. No, surely not, but that notion had placed a seed of doubt in her mind now and she would have to think hard about that, but later, she was busy at the moment. Turning back to her diaries, she started to read one of her entries, but her mind wandered again, this time thinking of her parents. They had left her some inheritance money when they had died, and that too helped her to be able to come to this sweet little cottage for a while. At the beginning, she had decided to invest her inheritance money and it had paid off, so now she was going to use some of that money to pay for the rent, utility bills and for the food etc. When she was married to Colin, she had offered to let him use the money when he had got his first promotion with the company, to use it for learning extra courses she had told him, but he wouldn't hear of it. He really had been a stubborn man when he had put his mind to something. Belinda stood and walked out onto the back porch, letting a tear run down her cheek as she looked up at the sky that was now turning a brilliant red with streaks of orange and yellow, God she did miss him. Shivering slightly, she wrapped her arms around herself as it was getting quite cool, but she found it hard to take her eyes from the sky as the colours shimmering through the atmosphere were hypnotising. She could have stayed out there all night but she still had work to do so she turned and walked back into the cottage, closing the door behind her.

     All her friends were busy with their own lives to question any plans that she might have made to be away for the next 6 months, even her friends she had shared her last night with hadn't been too concerned when she announced her plans of migrating up north for a while. She didn't feel neglected by that thought though, she knew they cared, but now and again, she did wish that there was that certain person in her life who would love her, love her forever. Colin had promised to do that, but sometimes promises couldn't be kept. If there was such a person as God, he had to answer to a lot of things that were going on down here. And come judgement day, she would be the first in line when it came to telling him a thing or two.

     The next day was fulfilling as far as getting a lot of writing done; saving her work and shutting the computer down, she took her memory stick and placed it in the top drawer of her desk, along with another backup copy that she always made. She sat back and laughed quietly to herself at her accomplishments so far, she had completed the first chapter of her first story, and it felt really good. Looking outside, the trees were swaying in the breeze letting her know that spring was indeed still holding on for dear life. She decided to go for a walk to clear her mind of all the labour she had done the last several hours, as she found it very taxing on her brain. Her head was hurting and she wasn't sure if it was from being at the computer for so long without a break or the strain of putting into words her life experiences, recreating them into a story setting, maybe a bit of both. She went into the kitchen and retrieved her coat from the coat hook in the corner and fastened up the buttons. The sun was shining slightly and it looked appealing to her to be outside for a while, but the wind was blowing, and she knew from her walk yesterday that there wasn't as much shelter from the cool breeze here as there was in the city. That didn't matter though, the fresh air would do her good, it definitely smelt nicer, unstained from all the pollutants that were in the city, and most pleasingly pleasant with all the different fragrances from the flowers that grew nearby. Maybe with the fresh air she might be able to get some inspiration as to how to start the next chapter of her story. There were all sorts of ideas running through her mind and maybe it was because she had been deep in thought, that she didn't see the car speeding around the tight bend at the end of the lane, but the shear terror on the young driver's face said it all. Belinda tried to cry out, but the horror that had enveloped her body had taken her voice from her. The young man didn't swerve in time to miss ramming the car into a stone wall at the side of the road, toppling the bricks onto Belinda, crushing her underneath.

Chapter Six

John lay down on his bed and felt apprehension come over him, he wanted to see Belinda again with all his heart, but his head kept shoving a different thought his way. 'You don't want to see her mate, she isn't real, well your relationship isn't real with her. Get a grip on yourself and pull yourself together lad. "**She isn't real and this has to stop**." he shouted. Lifting his hand to his head, he rubbed his forehead roughly, trying to ease the pain that was threatening to approach. He knew he was starting with a pounding headache, more like a hammer attacking his head really but he was also aware of his heart beating wildly, anxiety and excitement souring through his body like wildfire. John got up from his bed swiftly and started to walk around his bedroom. He could feel his muscles tensing up as he shrugged his shoulders, swinging his arms trying to release the knots that were tightening. He swept his hand through his hair as he sat back down on the edge of his bed knowing that the whole situation was getting ridiculous, he should be going out and finding someone real and alive to love and cherish. Not getting all enthralled, apprehensive, worried, excited and ecstatic all at the same time about his dream date. John chuckled out loud as that indeed was a true observation. He lay down once again; his breathing heavy and his heart thumping like a fighter opposing to being trapped in his body by his ribs, wanting to escape its prison to beat freely and contentedly, without restraint. John closed his eyes and waited for sleep to come. Would she be there? Was she waiting for him?

He was immediately in the woods a few feet from the waterfall. She wasn't stood under it this time, but was by his side, looking into his face with such love that instantly his heart burned in his chest with affection.

'He's here,' she thought sensing relief souring through her body, taking the frightening ache from her heart. She had been looking for him for what seemed like ages and as soon as he appeared, she instinctively threw her arms around his neck, pulling him close. Her eyes sparkled with slivers of lightening silver from the immovable desire that her body was expressing and the electricity that was evident was like a rocket at a fireworks display exploding inside them both. It wasn't just the sexual connection that was there, there was something distinctly different as well, there was a need to feel entwined mentally as well as physically and this was drawing them together with feelings of peace and harmony in their consciousness. Emotions were overwhelming John and he thought that at any moment now, his heart wouldn't be able to contain it all and that he would just disintegrate. He brought his mouth down to hers and kissed her with such an understanding that he felt a longing, wanting, not just for her body but for her as a person, for her whole being. Both their souls felt like they were joining together and it seemed as if at one time they were one person, somehow separating and upon meeting up joined back together as one.

His tongue explored her lips, tasting the sweetness of them and then requesting to delve deeper, asking her with his tongue to gain permission and acknowledging his desire, she parted them just enough for him to sweep his tongue in and enter her. He delved deeper into her, feeling her warmth and her tenderness and as she moved her mouth to accept him, he greeted her tongue with his. His hands moved over her body and they shook as he stroked down her back and across her bottom, she felt like utter perfection.

She stopped kissing him and pulled away slightly and as she looked up at him, she saw his eyes grow dark with longing and his breathing ragged just like hers. She tugged at his shirt and lifted it out of his trousers for the need to feel his skin next to hers was profoundly intense. She slid her hands up inside and across his chest, kneading his nipples slightly with her fingertips and feeling him flinch at this touch of intimacy. He was beautiful to caress and she could feel his muscles tensing and his shivers of delight as she moved her hands over him. John closed his eyes, giving a slight groan as his whole body shuddered. 'Oh God!' thought John, 'does this woman know what she's doing to me?' A rush of fire was souring through his veins just like you see on TV with a fire in a forest growing rapidly out of control. She could feel his arousal touching her stomach, growing and expanding with each beat of his heart. She slid her hands around to his back and pulled him close, so close that she could feel her breasts against his chest, her nipples growing taut as contact was made with her lips to his. John entwined his hand in hers and walked her over to the waterfall.

"I've wanted to do this since I first set eyes on you again," he whispered softly to her as they both stepped under the descending water, allowing the cool droplets to inflame their enraging passion even more. John shivered, but he knew he was not shivering because of the water being cold, he actually didn't even feel the coolness of the water, the heat emanating from both their bodies as they caressed and embraced each other. John pulled her close and planted kisses from her cheek down to her throat and heard her emit a whimper of a cry, he had never felt like this before, so much energy colliding and combining together as one. As he kissed her neck he looked down and saw her breathing growing faster and her chest rise and fall more rapidly with each passionate kiss. He pulled away slightly from her, watching the water falling down over the exposed swell of her breasts, observing the droplets run down, soaking her clothes making the fabric cling to her, sensing its need to touch her naked flesh and showing him once again the beauty of her body. Oh God! An electric impact riveted through him and he had to take a step back to steady himself. He glanced down at her body seeing that the cool water, clinging to her blouse had caused her nipples to stand to attention, the wetness pulling the material closely to her showing that she wasn't wearing a bra, manifesting to him how petite and succulent her breasts were.

John moved forwards and took her again in his arms as he wanted to love her forever and he knew he was hers for the taking. He lifted one of his hands to a breast and took the fullness in his hand as he lowered his head down, pulling gently at her erect nipple through her blouse with his teeth. Belinda threw her head back and cried out with delight. John groaned with her realising that the pleasure that he was able to give her made him more erotically ecstatic than ever. Belinda was intensely responsive to his caresses with an almost unwavering desire and as he slowly unbuttoned her blouse and drew it across her shoulders. He focused on her succulent breasts, his heart beating so fast that it could have been mistaken for a runaway train.

She needed more, More, MORE, she grabbed his shirt ripping it off his back as she threw it to the ground, crushing herself against him, her hands on his chest, stroking downwards to his stomach, slowly and tenderly and as they kissed, she used her fingers to caress his lower stomach just above the belt of his trousers. Unclasping his belt, she snapped open the button and ran a finger down the zip of his trousers, hearing John take in a gasp of air and moaning. Slowly her hand moved down inside his trousers to caress his arousal. John trembled, wrenching her hand away.
"Oh God no," he gasped. "I won't be able to last if you touch me like that." As he lifted her hands above her head, he drew them together and held them both in one hand. With the other hand, he slowly stroked down along the side of her body, lifting up her skirt as he moved his hand further up and caressed the top of her thigh, feeling the warmth and softness of her skin.

Belinda, letting frustration get the better of her and knowing her skirt was getting in the way, pulled one hand free from John's grip and undid the clasp at the back, letting it fall to the ground. John placed his hand between her legs, stroking her fairness over the top of her panties as Belinda wrapped a leg around his back, making it easier for him to explore her most intimate secret place. Upon hearing the little noises that Belinda made had John fighting for breath and as she gasped for fulfilment, pulling at his trousers, John threw them off with urgency. He gently moved down, withdrew her panties slowly and at the same time kissed her breasts and stomach, letting his tongue probe her curves and delicate skin as the water rushed in his way, mixing the water with her scent, creating droplets of elixir. Throwing themselves against the rock that shaped the structure at the back of the waterfall, John grabbed Belinda around her waist and lifted her up, letting her wrap her legs around his waist so that she was up off the ground. He leaned into her as she clenched her legs tightly around his body while he suckled one of her breasts and entered her slowly, making them both tremble with desire. John moved slowly, rocking back and forth whispering

Belinda's name and as he lifted his head, their lips met crushing together. She held onto his shoulders driving herself back and forth in unison with him until at last a rush of feelings flooded them both and they came to a perfect unconditional fulfilment. They both collapsed against the wall, their bodies beating so fast and loud that even the sound of the water couldn't stop them from hearing each other's hearts.

John held her against his chest stoking her hair and with Belinda's arms wrapped around his waist, she held him really tight, afraid that if she let go she would lose him. 'Was she crying now? Were those tears that were falling down her face against his beating heart? No it couldn't be,' he thought, 'it must be the water from the waterfall because why would she be crying after such an experience as this?'

"Are you OK," he gently asked her, lifting her chin to look at him. Searching her face he realised that she had been crying.

"I'm just so happy, I don't want this to end. I want us to be forever." It was as if she was pleading with him not to go away, ever. He wiped the tears from her face and smiled at her.

"Why are you here Belinda?" he said looking deep into her eyes. "I need to know what's going on" why was she in his dreams? and what was this power she held over him? Did she know the answers to all of this? or was she the same and totally unaware of the reasons for what was going on. Belinda smiled a beautiful smile, one that made John's heart ache with such a need to protect her and love her. He gripped her tightly to him afraid also to let her go.

'What did he mean by that question?' She wondered. 'Doesn't he know I'm the woman who loves him.' Belinda placed a hand on the side of his cheek and closed her eyes. Then she was gone.

Chapter Seven

'Oh Go, that's it, this has to stop, it's killing me,' thought John as he sat in his kitchen drinking some water, trying to quench his thirst and dampen his dry throat. That dream had been so real and powerful, even up to the point of them making love under the waterfall. It had seemed so real to John that when he had awoken, he was actually saturated with sweat and with the lingering scent and desire that lovemaking usually causes. He also had the same tiredness as he would have had, if he'd actually made love to her, here in reality. He was extremely tired, but at the same time he felt extraordinarily refreshed and for the rest of the night, John slept like a baby. Not waking up even once.

The next day at work was exhilarating because he managed to get a lot of work done that he'd not been able to concentrate on at all over the past few days. Peter called into John's office and propped himself against the desk where John was sat.
"You coming for a game of pool and darts tonight John?" he asked him. John looked up and just shrugged his shoulders feeling a panic in his chest, an ache coming from deep in his heart. There was no way he was going to miss any more time with Belinda than he would have to because her love was all that he needed in his life and he wanted to spend as much time with her as possible. He was about to decline the invitation and go straight home, but looking at Peter who was a good friend, changed his mind and smiled saying that he would go.
"After all," he grinned, "I need to get you back for the £15 you won off me last week." Peter stood and went to the door.
"You'll never be able to beat me at darts mate, and you know it," he stated laughing as he walked out of the office. It was silly to put his life on hold just for a woman who was after all only a figment of his imagination and although he knew it to be right, it still hurt.

The evening with his mates was great, better than he expected although he always did enjoy their sense of humour and he could feel himself relaxing more and more and laughing back with them at their somewhat funny jokes as the evening wore on.
"Come on then, tell us about this mystery woman that you've got stashed away somewhere." They said trying to get John to open up. How could he do that, there was no woman to talk of, not really. Wanting to change the subject, he rose from his seat.
"Right lads, my round, what does everyone want?"
"Good way to avoid the question mate," they commented, but as always it had done the trick. There was no better way to distract his mates than to offer them a drink from the bar and for him to pay too.

Later on, they had all said their goodbyes after the owner of the pub had threatened to throw them out if they didn't leave. Andrew, who ran the pub was a good man and a good friend to them and he knew that every time the lads came in, he would have to throw them out at closing time, but that was what was expected from a landlord, right! It was always all in fun, a ritual between the lads and the landlord. Andrew liked it that the lads wanted to stay longer, he did get a lot of business out of them and found it funny when he had to remind them that they had a life outside of the pub, which is why he didn't mind obliging the lads, it had become a ritual for them all.

"You must be feeling a lot better this evening." Peter said. "You've actually enjoyed yourself this time, that must be a first for what, at least 2 or 3 months?" Peter slapped his friend's back and they both laughed. John knew what had brought about this change. 'Belinda'. She was all that was needed to brighten up his life and she had done wonders for his soul last night.

"Yeah, it was great pal, maybe I won't wait as long next time." He wanted to make sure that Peter didn't feel like he was taking his friendship for granted because he wasn't. He appreciated everything that his mate did for him. As he left his friend and walked up the steps to his apartment, he whistled and quickened his pace, eager to get inside and to what lay ahead. This was absolutely stupid, a woman from a dream improving his attitudes to life, but what the hell, if that's what it took, then he wasn't going to complain. He hadn't felt as good as this in a long time, ever since Catherine had left him and cleaned out their joint bank account as well. He had given that woman 5 of the best years of his life and how did she repay him but by running off with all his money. It probably wouldn't have hurt as much if there'd been a man involved, but for her to run from him with nothing else on her mind but his money was almost too much to bear, at the time anyway. At least now, Belinda was taking some of that pain away and loving her came as easy as it could get, it was almost as natural as breathing, eating and sleeping, natural but also essential for his life to carry on.

Last night had been the most sensual encounter that he had ever had, not just because he had made love with her, but because the whole of his being had been taken by her and he had become hers to command. Anything she wanted she could have and he would be there to give it to her, love her, care for her and even give his life to her if that's what she wanted.

The nights when she didn't appear in his dreams, John awoke shivering, wet with perspiration and calling her name. He knew he was obsessed with her, but there was nothing that he could do about it.

A couple of days later, Peter ran after John as he left for work and walked by the side of him, matching his pace.
"I know I played a joke on you with Cheryl last time, I'm sorry mate about that, it won't happen again."
"You bet your life it won't pal" snorted John as they carried on walking. John stopped, slowly turning to face his friend, who had that silly look on his face again.
"Oh no, I am not doing it."
"What do you mean? I haven't said anything yet." answered Peter sniggering. John started walking once again and sighed heavily as Peter caught up with him.
"Who is it this time, Peter?" he asked before his friend had a chance to say anything.
"I'm glad you asked mate," he said as he wrapped his arm around John's shoulder and pulled him to his side. "Sharon has a friend at work who is single, beautiful and who has a great personality."
"Then why isn't she already hooked up?"
"Well she has just finished with her boyfriend and is in need of cheering up, if you know what I mean." he said nudging John in the ribs with his fist.
"That means that she'll be on the rebound mate, clingy as hell, no thanks."
"No, no, just out for a bit of fun, honest." he said grinning. They both carried on walking until they arrived at John's apartment. It was great that he'd been able to find a place so close to his work, as he enjoyed the exercise and thought that there was enough pollution in the world without adding to it with exhaust fumes.
"Look Peter, if I go on this one date, just this one time, will you get off my back?"
"For sure mate." replied Peter slapping John on his back. Walking back to the office with his car keys jingling in his hand, Peter thought out loud and laughed.
"He won't know what's hit him."
That night as John pulled up to the address that Sharon had rung through an hour before, John was having second thoughts. But he couldn't go back on this date now, he may not want to see anyone, especially since Belinda, but he wasn't about to hurt the woman's feelings. All he was going to do was to take her out to dinner and straight back home, letting her know in the nicest possible way, that this was a one and only date, after all there's no harm in that, and when he saw Belinda again, he would tell her all about it. He loved her too much to keep any kind of secrets from her. John laughed out loud, 'What the hell, Belinda is just dreams,' he thought, shaking his head.

As he knocked, he glanced in at the window to the side and saw a shadow move across towards the front of the door. Straightening his jacket, the door opened and John looked into the face of very beautiful woman.

And, Oh my God, what was she wearing? a negligee perhaps, although there wasn't enough material to call it anything. It was so low and so short and so see through, there wasn't anything left for the imagination anyway. All of a sudden, she grabbed him by his tie and pulled him into the house, spinning him around, as she closed the door and leaned against it so that his only means of escape had been sealed off.

"Hi," she said, "My name is Hope." and with this realisation, John's eyes grew wide and then it dawned on him what Peter had done, once again. He could feel the heat rising up his body. 'God, what was he going to do now.'

"Look, eh... Hope, I... I think there has been a misunderstanding here." stuttered John. Hope took a step towards him and threw out a hand, grabbing John very unexpectedly in the place meant only for intimacy and making him jump a foot or two into the air.

"I don't think so," she said. "Hmm, very nice." She let go of him and walked into the living room. John darted for the door and tried to open it, realising at once that she had locked it when she'd leaned against it and had taken the key. Turning around to look at her, she waved the key in front of him and slid it into her cleavage. John groaned. 'Oh no,' he thought, 'I'll kill him,' her breasts were big enough for him to be looking for the key for the next 5 years before he would find it.

"If you want it that bad, big boy, you'll have to come and get it." she said laughingly with a gleam in her eyes. John walked over to Hope and with a straight face held out his hand.

"I don't know what Peter or anyone else for that matter has said to you. But I don't go in for this sort of thing, so just hand over the key and I'll be on my way." Hope took a step closer to him and pressed her breasts against his extended hand, making John take a step back and dropping his hand back to his side as if it had been burnt.

"Like I said, if you want the key, you'll have to get it," she said with an evil glint in her eyes. John took a deep breath and stood just looking at her. Should he or shouldn't he? If he did put his hand in there to find the key, that might give her some idea that he was game, but if he didn't, how was he going to get out of the house. Maybe if he talked to her for a while, she would see sense and give him the key. Although looking at her, he didn't think that would work. Hope walked into the kitchen and swayed her flimsy gown around as she went.

"Have a seat and relax John," she said as she came back in with some drinks in her hands, seems like she was already prepared, as she wasn't gone more than a few seconds.

John wasn't finding this funny any more and could feel his temper starting to rise. Although he wasn't the kind of a person to shout at a lady, he didn't see what option he had.

"I don't want a drink thank you, if you'll just let me have the key, I'd like to go now." as he announced his wish to leave, he realised he had raised his voice more than he meant to and had made Hope flinch slightly.

She placed the drinks down onto the coffee table and looked at John, he could see the confusion in her eyes, after all this wasn't her fault.
"Your friend said you would be willing, why don't you try me, I'll help you relax all those muscles you have." she said trying to sound nonchalant.
"No thanks," said John more quietly this time as he walked back over to her and again extended his hand. Hope grinned, it seemed like she thought it to be an invitation once again.
"If you're so desperate to leave, you know where the key is." She stepped even closer to him, took hold of his hand and pressed it onto her cleavage. With that John closed his eyes and reached down to retain the key.

Sat in the car a few minutes later, managing to escape the clutches of Hope and after peeling her hands away from his buttocks and other parts of his anatomy, he started up the engine and drove home. Once he got there, he laughed purely out of relief, this was so typical of Peter and Sharon, the practical jokers that they were. It would have been funny if it hadn't been for the fact that he was already taken. But they hadn't known that, if they had, then they wouldn't have done what they did. They were good friends, and wouldn't have jeopardised a relationship that he had with anyone, but Peter also knew that even if he wasn't seeing anyone, he didn't go to strange women's homes and do the business. 'Peter must be roaring with laughter now,' he thought. After hanging up the phone and leaving an explicit message on his mate's answering machine, saying he would preach to them both later on about their evil ways, he felt much better and went to get a whiskey from the cabinet in the kitchen.

During the night, as he and Belinda were sat by the stream talking about anything and everything, John told her about Peter's intervention into his life. Belinda started to laugh and seemed to find it extremely funny.
"It wasn't funny," exclaimed John smiling, surprised and pleased that Belinda could take it so lightly, considering such a short time ago, he had had his hand down another woman's cleavage.
"What did she do when you tried to get the key?" asked Belinda trying her hardest not to laugh.
"She grabbed my bum, gave me a fright I can tell you." John lay back onto the grass with his hands behind his head, looking at Belinda. "She nearly gave me a heart attack. It was all I could do to get out of there with my innocence intact."
Belinda laughed out loud.
"Yeah, right, you innocent." She leaned over and started to tickle him, this caused a stirring in John and he pulled Belinda on top of him and tickled her until she was crying out for mercy. It was getting easier whenever Belinda or he disappeared from each other, because they knew that it wasn't the end and they would soon be back in each other's arms the next night.

Chapter Eight

A couple of weeks later, people at work were all talking about the big change that had come over John, they knew there was something very different about him. He was still the best Architect that the company had, but they did notice that he always came to work tired, they had definitely noticed that, but yet he was sublimely happy.
"Hi John" said Peter. "What's up?"
John turned to see his friend enter his office so he put down the documents that he was reading and turned his attention to his friend.
"You've been up a lot at night, have you?" Peter winked at John and smiled. John leaned back against the chair and stretched his legs out and smiled. Just thinking about Belinda put a big smile on his face, but it also put a deep uncontrollable pain in his heart because of the unreality of it all.
"Peter, you have a one track mind, you know that, right?" replied John. He couldn't tell anyone about Belinda, they wouldn't understand at all, they would think that he was crazy, take him off to the asylum quick smart. He did himself think at the beginning of going to see a doctor. The doctor might be able to tell him why he was dreaming so much about Belinda and why it seemed so real, why he had become so obsessed with her? It felt just the same as loving someone whom was real in his life like a lover, friend and companion should be, but he couldn't go to see a doctor, could he? The doctors would think he was crazy, maybe depressed and try and give him anti-depressants or something like that. He also didn't want to think that there was some cause to these dreams that maybe the doctor could cure. If he was cured, then the dreams would stop, and no way did he want these dreams to stop. Ever!
"Been up late drawing plans for the Nicholson file, that's all" replied John. Peter propped his tall lean body against the desk. This seemed to be Peter's favourite place to lounge in, in here or in any other room that had a desk.
"You need to get out and have some fun, why don't you come down to the pub with all the lads and see where the action is." John noticed that Peter's face looked almost serious.
"What is it with pubs and you?" grinned John. "You think all problems can be solved by going to the pub with the lads." John had said that with such disbelief that Peter threw his head back and laughed out loud.
"That's where the women are John, if you hadn't noticed. They come down to the pubs to be picked up, loved, pampered and swooned over."
He knew that Peter was joking about the women, at least for himself anyway. He was totally and happily married to Sharon.
He was a great friend though, but he didn't want anyone poking around in his life, besides he did have a lot of work to catch up on. His mind hadn't been on any of it as it should have been and he was a little behind with things.

"Give me 2 or 3 more hours and maybe I'll be finished for today. Then perhaps............" Looking up from his work, John saw Peter smiling at him.
"Okay Peter, I'll go to the pub with you, talk about women and act all manly," he said joking and sarcastically. Again Peter laughed at John's wit. Maybe that would satisfy them that he was okay and once his mates were satisfied then he would be able to go home to relax and concentrate on Belinda.
"That's the way mate." replied Peter as he walked out of the office. John opened up the document he had been concentrating on and focused his attention back to his work.

When he next looked at the clock, it was almost 6.30pm, time for him to call it a day. He had better hurry if he was to spend some time with the lads before meeting Belinda. John stood up and then sat back down into his chair laughing, but it wasn't a laugh of something comical, it was a laugh of desperation. "Just listen to yourself again man, 'before meeting Belinda', what are you thinking of? what is going on?" John said aloud almost shouting his thoughts as he tried to make sense of his life. Throwing all his work into his briefcase, he sighed and headed out of the office and onto his apartment. Once he arrived home, he quickly showered and shaved, throwing on some slacks and a polo shirt and whilst he was combing his hair, he checked his messages on his answering machine, there was just one from Peter.
"Just to remind you about tonight pal, just in case you had forgotten on your way home from the office." Typical of Peter smiled John, he knew that he had a good friend there, irritating, annoying and stubborn, but a good friend.

He enjoyed being with his friends that evening, playing a few games of darts and pool, joined in also with a few rounds of beer, that always went down well. He usually drank a couple of beers when he went out with the lads, but he never had been much of a pub person or even a drinker, he knew his limit, but all his friends tonight had seemed to think that he needed more than a few and the beer had gone straight to his head. 'I bet they're deliberately trying to get me drunk, so that I'll spill the beans about my mysterious woman,' he'd thought. Peter had to almost carry John home and as soon as he got into apartment and within seconds of lying down, he was asleep. Letting the latch down on the door, he slammed it shut, trying it first to make sure that it was locked before he went home, laughing.

He was back in the meadow where Belinda was waiting for him. She ran straight into his arms and put her head against his chest, she loved the warmth that his body radiated and the smell, she took in a deep breath and sighed ecstatically, if this was heaven then this is where she wanted to be for the rest of her life.

John lowered his head as he stroked her hair to kiss the top of her forehead. She looked as radiant as ever, no matter what she was wearing. This was strange, he wasn't drunk in his dream and his mind was a clear as if he hadn't consumed any alcohol at all, at least that's one good thing about dreams, he didn't want his thoughts to be impaired by alcohol, especially tonight as he'd decided that he would not let his bodily lusts get the better of him. He held Belinda's hand and began to walk with her along the side of the river. They didn't talk for what seemed like ages, just held each other's hands, walking and smiling at one another. This was so perfect.
'He's here with me,' she thought 'and it feels like the most natural thing in the world to be walking along with him, holding his hand. It doesn't matter that we aren't having a conversation at all. Just being together is enough.' She looked at him and smiled. His eyes greeted her and lit up when he smiled back making them sparkle even more.
'Was his heart beating so fast because of wanting her or because he was immensely happy?' he couldn't decide which was making him so ecstatic and happy, his lust for her body or his lust for her companionship, probably both.

John gazed up at the sky. 'Were all dreams like this with the flawless weather, perfect blue sky with brilliant white clouds lining it and to top it all, the sun's rays shining down to give warmth to the mother earth. If only this dream could last forever,' he thought and as he looked at Belinda, his heart ached once more, she was the most beautiful and sensuous woman in the world. But what world was he thinking about? Where exactly was this world that they were both in, was it in his dreams because he never remembered ever having dreams as real as these, ever. They stopped walking at an old Oak tree that had a pillow of brightly coloured leaves around the bottom of it all clumped together. The leaves seemed to have been placed there just for them and as John pulled her gently to the ground beside him, he couldn't help himself, he had to kiss her. Coming up for air with their breathing ragged and harsh, they sat together and held each other tightly, as if afraid to let go in case either one of them disappeared. They talked for what seemed like hours although most of the talking came from John telling Belinda of his work and of his friends in the office and how they wondered what he did every evening instead of going out with them any more.

Looking towards Belinda he reached for her hand and kissed it, holding her hand close to his heart. "I want to spend as much time as I can with you, I guess that's being selfish, but hey, a man has to dream," with that last comment, John grinned a wicked grin at Belinda and drew his mouth down to hers, closing in for the kill as they say. After what seemed like forever, they parted lips and John, shaking from the increasing passion that was developing once again, took a deep breath.

"Tell me about yourself Belinda, what happens when you leave here, what do you do with your life?" John hoped and prayed that these dreams were somehow another reality, one that had some way infringed on his sleeping world and brought him here. He couldn't bear to think that when he awoke, Belinda didn't continue to exist somewhere, anywhere else, as long she was a living, breathing creature, he could cope with that. He desperately needed for her to be someone that he could really love and not be ashamed of, because sometimes he did feel embarrassed of the love that had matured and grown in his heart, maybe for only an illusion. Sometimes when the lads were talking about their perfect woman and the fantasies that they had, he had longed to join in with them and tell them all about Belinda, but these dreams weren't in the same league as men's normal fantasy dreams. He so much wanted his Belinda to be here, to be real.

John knew that this was a dream, and that he was asleep, so............ 'If I am acknowledging that Belinda is not real,' he thought, 'then it has to be real, doesn't it?' Did that make sense, or was his mind playing tricks on him? After all he was asleep, so anything could happen. Is that how it works. Had he so much control over his dreams that he could make anything happen. Is this why Belinda was here with him, because he was so lonely that he had to dream her up to make his life complete. All he knew was that he was content at work, and he had some good friends whom he saw down at the local. He even knew that there were some of his women friends who would drop everything to be at his side for an evening of wining and dining. Although if he was honest about it, before his dreams of Belinda started, he did often awake during the night and find himself wishing there was someone next to him that he could just hold on to, not just anyone but someone special. Not always to make love to, although that would have been lovely too, but just someone to be there to comfort him and hold him as much as he would comfort and hold them. Although now he was experiencing true passion and adoration, he wanted nothing else, but only with one person and she was unobtainable.

Belinda, sensing that John's mind was elsewhere had left him to his own thoughts for a while, but after a few minutes, touched his chin and turned his head so that he was looking at her.
"What happens when you leave, where do you go? Belinda stared at Colin wish she could answer his questions, but quite honestly, she didn't know herself.
"The only thing that I remember is when I am here with you, I feel complete as though nothing else matters anyway. I don't really remember what I was doing immediately prior to being here or after, but I do feel as if there is something, else."

She went on to tell John about Colin and how she had at one time loved him, how he had helped her when life had dealt her a callous hand and she hadn't known which direction to take or even how to get over it.
"He taught me how to trust again, how to love without fear or regret, and believe with total certainty that his love wouldn't wither and die."
"Do you still love him now?" asked John, not really wanting to listen to what she had to say about her love for this other man, but needing to hear it anyway.
"I will always love Colin, but not in the same way as I love you. It was very different, the love I had for him was more of a contentment to love a good man who loved me back, and who would love me always, never giving me cause to doubt his faithfulness, especially concerning my feelings. He would never hurt me, he was my saviour back then, but his and my time has passed now, and I've moved on. There never was that special connection although at times and I had wished that there had been, because he was and is very special to me and he always will be. But you and me, well that connection is there with everything......"
Looking up at him she gripped his chin slightly tighter so that she could pull him down and kiss his tender, loving lips. John knew she had put that last part in sensing his fear of what she might say. He also perceived that Belinda was close to tears, seeing the hurt look in her eyes of not being in full control of her life at the moment and being in total confusion. He wished that he could help her somehow but hell, he couldn't even control what was going on in his own life, what could he possibly do to help this woman whom he was deliriously in love with, if he couldn't even help himself. Breaking from her kisses, he looked around him seeing some buttercups growing at the side of where they were sat. He picked one up, smiled and gave it to Belinda. She chuckled, he was so loving at times that it made her heart flutter.
"Well thank you kind Sir." She said grinning back at him and leaning forwards, she placed a soft, tender kiss on his lips once again, her kiss sending shivers down John's spine. Don't think about it mate, you promised yourself that you were going to behave yourself this time and that you were both just going to talk so John took a deep breath to steady his racing heart and took hold of Belinda's hand. Pressing it to his lips, he kissed it, stroking his tongue along each finger, one at a time. He heard Belinda gasp air in quickly and could see her eyes light up and sparkle as she licked her lips slowly and lusciously. He knew what he was doing but he couldn't seem to stop so to take some of the tension away that was building up in both of them for some serious lovemaking, John nibbled her fingers and when that made her laugh he proceeded to tickle her. They found themselves rolling around in the grass laughing and when they stopped, both out of breath, John reached over to Belinda and took a piece of grass out of her hair using it as a tickling stick on her nose, she screwed up her nose and pulled out her tongue at him. God, everything that she did was sexy, how did she manage it?

He tenderly leaned over and kissed her nose, then each eyelid one at a time, moving across to her ears and nibbling them. Hearing the moans from her throat made John's arousal stir. 'God help me,' he moaned. Taking his mouth back to hers, he took hold of her inviting tongue with his teeth and Belinda found this so comical that she fell back laughing once again. John took Belinda in his arms and they lay against each other and before they knew it, they were fast asleep.

After what had seemed a long time, John awoke, glanced over at Belinda as she lay on the grass and saw her looking up at the sky. She was watching the clouds darken as they moved across the horizon.
"You Okay?" He asked.
"Hmm, wonderful, and you?"
"I haven't had so much fun in a long time, well not with a woman anyway." He commented winking at her. John stood upright, pulling Belinda into his arms and kissed her gently on the lips before continuing on with their walk along the side of the river, talking about anything and everything. If this was what dreaming was like, he didn't want to wake up ever again. He was quite happy to stay here with Belinda and never go back to the waking world, if he was in control of his own dreams then maybe he could stay, never to wake to loneliness ever again. Belinda pointed over to the other side of the river at a couple of squirrels playing by an old tree trunk. John stepped around to the back of her and wrapped his arms around her waist, pulling her into his body and resting his chin on the top of her shoulder. Having her body pulled so close to his own, he groaned, very aware of his arousal pressing into the small of her back. He had to take his mind of this burning sensation that was threatening to take over his body, but how. He turned her around still holding onto her waist, God, he couldn't resist her any longer and he had to kiss her no matter how his body reacted. Pulling her closer still, his lowered his head and slowly touched her lips with his. Gently first letting his tongue feel the softness of her mouth, lying on more pressure as his yearning increased. Belinda tilted her head back giving John access to her neck and throat, his lips feeling the vibration of each beat of her heart, beating faster with each kiss. He placed his hands on her rear and pressed her into him, letting her feel the reaction that he was experiencing from their kiss. Belinda was gone, all caution thrown to the wind this time, maybe they had only wanted to talk at first, but that time had now passed. She called his name as he raised his head and pressed his mouth hard and fast upon hers. The first drops of rain came to fall upon their faces, cool and refreshing against their skin and they could hear thunder in the distance and it seemed to be closing in on them. Belinda gasped as John swung her up into his arms and walked them over to the waterfall, clinging on as she placed her arms around his neck and rested her head against his shoulder, gently he lowered her down onto her feet, making sure that her body rubbed against his, slowly and provocatively, making her gasp for breathe even more.

"If we're going to get wet, I'd much prefer it under here," he said with a wicked grin on his face. The water fell upon them both, seeping through their clothes as they stood looking at each other, their hearts starting to race faster once again and their breathing growing more rapidly as the seconds pass. John looked at Belinda and stepped back. "I shouldn't have brought you under here." She stepped one pace towards him, pressed a finger to his lips feeling the heat emanate from his body. He shuddered as she brought her arms up and wrapped them around his neck, feeling his muscles tensing underneath his shirt. Looking up, she could see the sky getting hellishly dark and the rain was much heavier now, bouncing off the river like a dance of skipping fireflies. Belinda laughed as she put her hands over her ears as the thunder crashed and rumbled above them. Lightening rippled across the clouds like fire sweeping through a blanket of cotton wool. John pulled her close to him and felt his heart pound hard against his chest as he took her face in his hands and gently leaned forward to touch her lips with his. Belinda suddenly gave out a cry as she fell back against the rock face of the waterfall, she looked at John with an expression on her face that he had never seen before, a look of shear panic.

"Belinda, it's Okay," he shouted above the thunderous noise emanating from the sky above, wanting to calm her and comfort her. It was so dim and dark now that he couldn't make out her face properly as she was just a shadow between the sheets of water falling from the rocks above. She crouched down holding out a hand to John and as she called out his name she began to fade away.

"John, come find me." She pleaded. Belinda reached for him, then she just disappeared into thin air.

"What's happening?" John screamed out into the open expanse of the countryside around him. All of a sudden, a thought hit him like a tidal wave. He was still there, in the dream. When Belinda disappeared he usually woke up, so why wasn't he awake now. A sudden realisation came upon him and he fell down to his knees to where Belinda had been, never before feeling as much torment in his heart as he did at that moment. She had disappeared right before his eyes and John was left all alone. He stood up and shouted her name.

"Belinda, how do I find you, where do I go?" At that very moment, sheer terror enveloped him, he knew that in the pit of his stomach, that he had lost Belinda, that he would never see her again. He fell quiet, perfectly still as he lowered his head and closed his eyes.

Chapter Nine

Awake and fighting for breath, John stumbled out of bed, trying to calm his heart as he took some deep breaths, but that didn't help at all as it was still beating too fast, no doubt with the unquestionable fear of realising that his life had just ended. His body was trembling uncontrollably now and no matter how he tried to keep calm, he couldn't stop it. He walked unsteadily into the kitchen to get a drink of water. Letting the glass fall, it smashed as it landed into the base of the sink. He slid his body down against the cupboards onto the floor, drawing his knees up as he placed his hands over his face. He tried to keep the tears from falling, but to no avail.

All of a sudden a thought came to him, he realised that all he had to do was go back to sleep. Maybe she would be there and maybe this wasn't the end after all.
"Please be there Belinda, I need you so much," he cried out loud, no matter how hard he tried, he couldn't get back to sleep. "Calm done mate," he said trying to soothe himself, "breathe deeply and concentrate." When sleep did finally overcome him, it was only to be in short bursts, he would wake up time and time again throughout the night knowing that his soul had been searching and seeking for his love, but it had been in vain. Was this it then, was he destined to be alone for the rest of his life? For he would never love again, because when she went away, she took his heart with her.

At the hospital, all the alarms that were connected to Belinda started screaming and wailing, letting the staff know that something was horrifically wrong with her. The room was immediately full of doctors and nurses who'd appeared out of nowhere, obeying orders as they were being shouted, voices seemed to be coming from everywhere and people were moving around her tending to their duties and working very effectively together as a team, each knowing how to do their job and getting on with it, with such precision and accuracy that anyone would think they were on automatic pilot they knew a life depended on them keeping calm and coping with the situation at hand. The adrenaline of the staff in the room had reached an all-time high and once the doctors realised that Belinda was haemorrhaging inside, from an unforeseen injury that had been caused from the accident, they rushed her straight to theatre. It was touch and go for a while, but after 3 hours of surgery, the surgeon relaxed a little and asked the attending doctor to finish off by stitching up. The surgeon left the operating room and pulled his mask down over his face, wiping the well-earned sweat from his brow as he went to see the doctor who was in charge of Belinda's case.

"That was a close call, I would say, don't know why she hadn't haemorrhaged sooner. If she had been awake, she would have been able to tell us because of the pain that she would've been experiencing." announced the surgeon. "Have you found out who she is yet?"
"Not yet we haven't," replied her doctor. "We're thinking of letting some of the local and national papers do a story on her, maybe that will bring some unsuspecting relative out of the woodwork and realise that they haven't heard from her in a while."

Belinda was kept in the ICU unit to be on the safe side just in case something else cropped up that was unforeseen, but she recovered from the surgery with no problems, although she was still in a coma totally oblivious to what was happening to her. The doctors were unsure what was causing this medical state that she was in, although she'd had some head injury when she was brought in, they didn't think that it warranted her to be in a coma. All the swelling had gone down from her head injury and the brain scans showed that she was recovering well. It was as if she had lost the will to live. The nurses who attended her often spoke to her as though she could hear them as sometimes that had proven to be a satisfactory way of coaxing someone out of a coma, if a loved one was to speak to them every day. Since no one knew who Belinda was or any of her relatives or close friends, the nurses had taken it upon themselves to talk to her at least for a little while each day. After a few days, Belinda was well enough to be moved to a private room that was at the bottom of a ward and here the nurses were able to talk to her in private, sometimes bringing music in for her to listen to.

Each day, John went into work and tried very hard to concentrate, but there was no way he could focus on anything or on anyone who needed his attention about any of their work problems, He was respected and had earned himself a commendable reputation as someone who cared about what his clients wanted and what his fellow work mates required. He would do his best to see that everyone received the utmost attention when needed, but at the moment he felt unable to help anyone on anything. Hell, he couldn't even help himself at the moment and he'd already lost his temper at a few people that morning and that wasn't the way he normally was, especially at work, as he prided himself on being a calm and considerate person. So by lunchtime, he had given up trying to do any type of 'normal everyday work' and decided to go home. He told his Secretary he was taking some of his holiday time that was due to him effectively immediately.
"So I won't be in for the rest of the week Helen, all the clients that have been assigned to me for this week transfer to someone else will you, or tell them I'll be available next week. Can you manage to shift my workload around on such short notice, is that OK?"

He knew Helen worked really hard and had a lot of work to do already without him causing her any more trouble, but looking at her face, the concern that he felt left him.

"Don't worry John," she smiled. "I'll sort everyone out, you go and get some R & R," she blew a kiss to him as he left the office. Helen was one in a million all right, he was so glad to have a Secretary as good as her, his other colleagues knew that and sometimes envied him.

Once he was home, he threw his briefcase onto the floor by the side of the couch and went into the kitchen. Flicking the switch on the kettle, he rooted through the cupboards for some hot chocolate mix, he had seen some a couple of months ago when some of his friends had popped around. They had brought their daughter with them and John had made her some of his famous hot chocolate with little marshmallows in it. It had been a great success and upon leaving, the little girl was overheard saying to her dad that she wanted to come and visit the marshmallow man again, he smiled as he took a sip of the chocolate and went into the living room to relax. Sitting on the couch for just a few minutes might help and spreading his legs out in front of him, he picked up the local newspaper and scanned through it, not seeing much of anything interesting to read, he threw it back onto the coffee table. After finishing his chocolate he did feel considerably calmer, so maybe now he could fall asleep and dream of Belinda. He went into the bedroom and slackened his tie, drawing it up over his head as he sat on the edge of his bed, giving a downhearted sigh. Unbuttoning his shirt, he drew it down over his shoulders and threw it over the back of the chair. He untied his shoes and tossed them off with his socks. How he wished that she were real, how he wished that he was taking her with him onto the bed, not necessarily to make love but just to sleep. To be able to hold her against him and feel the love and warmth that radiated from her, to see her looking up at him and to see her smile that wonderful smile. When she had smiled at John before, he had seen all the love flowing from her and to feel all that love was a dream come true. If that was what true love was like, to have a woman love you so much that you could see nothing but love in her face when she looked at you, then John wanted that again, badly. When he lay down with his head rested against the pillow, his body started to shake with anticipation and also of the impending dread of what might not be there. He was shivering and it wasn't cold in his room at all, so what was the matter with him and why couldn't he keep calm? He closed his eyes and was asleep within minutes, Belinda being the last thing on his mind when he went to sleep and the first when he awoke. Awaking to find himself on his side curled up like a ball, he was aware straight away that he had not dreamed of her. A deep pain shot through to his core as his heart broke inside, he screwed up his face at the distress he felt and his gut tightened up with the pain. He knew in his soul that this would be no more, he had lost Belinda forever and he could feel it.

No matter how many times he succeeded to go to sleep, Belinda was never there, so a couple of days later when he was at his drawing table, looking at some plans that he had started on a couple of weeks ago and were in need of finishing, he thought back to University when architectural drawing wasn't his first actual passion, he got up from his seat and went upstairs into the spare room. Behind one of the closets was an old portfolio that he carried around when going for his interview to attend the University. Inside were drawings that he had done of people, portraits and full profiles of his friends and family and buildings such as churches, old farmhouses etc. His art tutor had encouraged him to take up architectural drawing when he had seen the detail that he had put into the buildings, saying that his talent would be best used in that direction. He had never looked back until now, all of a sudden he yearned for his old talent to come back out of hiding and decided to focus his mind on his old drawings for a while.

The next day, he went into the one and only craft shop that was situated in his small town and walked around until he eventually found what he was looking for. He paid for his items and left and when he got back to his apartment, he went straight into the spare bedroom. He wondered if he could concentrate enough to go back in time and bring all those drawing talents out into the open once again. He sat down on a chair that he had placed into the small narrow box room, even though he never had used this room, he had tried to make it comfortable enough just in case one of his friends had ever wanted to stay there. It was a very tiny room, with only enough space for a single bed, a chest of drawers, which most of the time he kept old bills and paper stashed away, and the recliner chair in which he now sat. He could have used his drawing table but this was much too personal to place these drawings with plans of buildings, they were not attached to anyone's heart, these drawings that he was going to do were. He took the drawing pad and rested it on his lap with a couple of fine tipped pencils that he had bought from the crafts shop. Relaxing back into the chair, he let it recline back so his legs were stretched out in front of him. Closing his eyes for a few minutes enabled him to get a clear picture of what Belinda looked like, he wanted every detail to be perfect. He began to draw, at first making lots of mistakes and cursing quite a few times, but eventually Belinda's face began to take form on the paper. He carried on putting pencil to paper without stopping, taking only time to eat and drink. Now and again he catnapped, only getting small amount of sleep necessary for his body to keep going. He wanted as many pictures as he could to remind him of her, thinking of all the different places they had been. There was the waterfall where he had first glimpsed her and in the meadow by the stream. He wanted to catch the different expressions that she'd had on her face, making all these memories come alive somehow.

Eventually though, his body alerted him to the need of some serious sleep, his eyes were dark and sunk deep into his head. He hadn't shaved in days and a dark bristly beard had grown making him look more rough and weary. How long had he been at this now, 2, 3 days perhaps. He put down his drawings and walked over to the bed, let his body fall heavily onto it and fell asleep. He slept for what seemed hours with the sun's rays pouring into the room when he awoke, making him squint and having to place his hand over his eyes until he adjusted to the brightness of the new day. Looking over at the clock, he realised he must have slept through the rest of the day yesterday and all the night as well. He got up off the bed and went into the kitchen for a cup of coffee. Lots of caffeine and food, that's what he needed, just the thing. For the next couple of days, John sat in the small room working on his pictures because to him, nothing else seemed to matter at the moment and he realised that finishing the drawings was foremost in his mind. He needed some sort of reminder of Belinda that he could look at so he plodded on drawing until at last, he sat with the finished products laid out on the bed. Looking at the pictures in front of him, looking closely at them, he knew in his heart that the pictures would probably make matters worse, but at that moment and until he was ready to let her go, he needed them. He studied the pictures carefully, satisfied that he had captured Belinda's dark flowing hair perfectly and her sparkling hazel eyes to a tee. She was indeed very beautiful. Wearily, John got up from the chair knowing for a fact that one day, he would have to come to terms with the unwelcome reality of it all. Belinda was gone and she was not coming back, but for a little while longer he wanted to pretend that she was still with him and that their love was real and would last forever.

Feeling satisfied at all his hard work he walked into the bathroom and took a good long look at himself in the mirror, noting that he was indeed in need of a shave and a long overdue soak in the bath. Maybe that would take some tension away. He ran the water in the tub and got undressed, wrapping a towel around his middle whilst he quickly shaved and then stepped into the warm soothing water, feeling his muscles relaxing straight away making him wonder why he hadn't done this earlier. So this was what women were always on about, having a soak in the bath that lasted hours to relax them, causing the men folk in their households to despair. John had never felt the need to do this before. He'd had lots of baths, even with company but he had never had one for the sole purpose of relaxation. He was usually too busy to indulge himself in that kind of leisurely activity. Afterwards, feeling quite refreshed and more like a human being he got something to eat and walked back into the spare room. What was he going to do with all these drawings, he needed somewhere to put them away from any preying eyes and safe from being lost.

Going back down to the crafts shop, he purchased an arts folder, one like students had to show their work to prospective employers or colleges and placing all the drawings in the folder would give him instant access to be able to look at them any time at all. Once home he closed up the folder with the drawings contained within and pushed it under the bed in the spare room. What was he to do now, should he try and go to back to work, was he ready for that? He didn't know. Bending down and reaching under the bed, he grabbed the folder, John got up and walked over to the door leading into the hallway of his apartment and taking his coat, he set the answering machine on by his phone. Slamming the door, he slung his coat over his shoulder and walked down to the car. Getting into the driving seat, he started the engine and proceeded the long drive to London and to the restaurant where he had last seen Belinda. As he walked into the reception area he opened up the folder containing the drawings of Belinda and took out the one that he had done of her sat by the side of the river and showed it around to the bar staff, hoping that someone might recognise her and be able to tell him where she lived or maybe where she worked. Exiting the place 10 minutes later and not getting any closer to finding anything about her, he got back into the car.. His next stop would be the nightclub where he had seen Belinda and her friends dance, but that was hopeless also, no one seemed to know who she was. He drove around the streets entering all the local pubs and showed Belinda's picture to anyone who might be able to tell him where she lived or at least her last name. Some of the local pubs said they had seen her now and again, but not for a while and didn't know her name or where she lived.

   Returning home in the early hours of the morning after hours of showing the drawing of Belinda around, he re-entered his home, placed the folder back under the bed and went into the kitchen to make himself a sandwich. He had drunk enough coffee that evening whilst he was out on his errand, but he was starving for food. Glancing at the clock, it was close to 3 am so he turned off all the lights, made sure that the door was locked and went to bed.

Chapter Ten

The next few days were the hardest as he couldn't sleep or eat very much. He knew he should get a hold of himself, but he was finding it too hard. He sometimes laughed at his thoughts, 'fancy going to pieces because of a few dreams.' All he seemed able to do was sit on the couch and look through his drawings of Belinda; he knew he shouldn't because the pictures were just prolonging the agony.

John heard a knock on the door and he wished whoever it was would go away and leave him alone. The banging on the door became louder and with it came an irritated voice.
"Come on John, I know you're in there". John knew instantly who it was, Peter his old friend.
"Your neighbour's seen you collecting your milk every morning", shouted Peter banging again on the door, even louder this time. John put the pictures back under the bed and went out into the living room towards the door. When he opened it, Peter took one look at him and his face grew grim.
"What's the hell's wrong with you? You look terrible", said Peter as he pushed past him into his apartment.
"Thanks for your concern, and I'm glad to see you too." said John turning round to face his friend.
"What sort of illness have you had?" John saw the room spin and suddenly his stomach turned and he felt overwhelmed with nausea. He stumbled towards the wall to hold himself upright as Peter grabbed hold of him and guided him into the living room.
"Right", he said. "You'd better tell me what's going on, considering I'm not leaving here until you do, or shall I call a doctor, because by the looks of you, you haven't". John knew that he needed to talk to someone, although he felt ashamed for going all to pieces because of Belinda, or should he say an imaginary Belinda. He got up slowly from the chair and walked into the spare bedroom and as he walked back out, he handed Peter the folder. As Peter opened it, pictures of Belinda came into view. He looked at the drawings, as John talked about his feelings for Belinda and about the dreams, Peter didn't say a word, he just glanced up at John now and again then back at the drawings. After he had finished spurting out his heart, he sat back against the chair and covered his face with his hands. Now he had done it, Peter would call the hospital immediately and tell them that he was sending someone to them and to get one of their padded cells ready. John laughed just thinking about it.
"I wish I could laugh about it man." Peter said producing out of him a heavy sigh, and placed the closed folder down onto the coffee table.
"John, look at me," he said. John took his hands down from his face, he sat up straighter glancing at his friend.

He could tell Peter looked disturbed and he could see the nervousness in his eyes as he tried to come to terms with his friend's despair. Looking deep in thought, Peter moved to sit closer to John.

"I don't know what's going on here pal, but you have to pull yourself together man."

"I know you must think I'm crazy, but I can't let go, and I can't stop feeling what I'm feeling." It felt good to actually talk about it at long last and he didn't care what his friend thought, so holding up his head, he looked right into Peter's eyes.

"I can't help it mate," replied John. "I know it's mad, but this feels so real to me, and not just real, but it feels so dam right as well. It was as though my dreams were another life that I was living as well as this waking one, they were both as real as each other, but now she's gone and I can't live with that." John cleared his throat as he went and sat over by the window, trying hard to control his emotions and stop them from exploding inside him. He leaned his body towards the window and looked at the world outside, he could see people going about their own business who were oblivious to the fact of occurrences happening around them that were shaking the very foundation of life itself. He turned around and looked at his friend who was still staring at him with a solemn face and troubled eyes.

"Don't look at me like that Peter," John said emotionally. "I need your help, not your pity, but not if you think I need a shrink as I'm not crazy, although if someone had told me what I have told you, I would think otherwise as well." John brushed his hand through his hair and Peter could see tears threatening to burst out of him like a leaking pipe ready to explode.

"Maybe talking about it to you will be just the help that I need to shake myself out of this hole that I'm in." John said glancing over at his confidant. Peter sighed as he stood at the window with his friend, taking a quick glimpse out seeing that the sun was just going down with the sky turning a burning red, he loved this time of day, as looking upon a sky like this, it made the world seem beautiful, the perfect place to be. Yet how could there be so many problems in people's lives. Peter didn't like seeing his mate hurt like this. But he really didn't know what to think about this situation that John was in. Was his friend having a nervous breakdown? was he going insane? and how could he help his friend? What the hell was he to do?

"Right," said Peter grabbing John and leading him into his bedroom.

"Get some clothes, go take a shower and get yourself ready." ordered Peter. John turned around and opened his mouth to protest, to tell him 'forget it.' But he closed it quickly as he could see the concern in his face and knew that it would be futile to refuse, his friend was trying to help and John wouldn't stop him.

"I'll give you half an hour, you should be ready by then," Peter said. He knew it wouldn't sort out this dilemma that his friend was in, but at least it would take his mind of it for a few hours.

Within the hour, they were eating a well need meal, Colin's body shouting for joy for at last, obtaining the nourishment it had so badly craved.

"I don't really want to go in there." commented John looking at his friend s they arrived at the local theatre. Peter just shrugged his shoulders.

"Tough, you're going in, so that's that." Peter didn't want to be hard on his friend. But he didn't know how to react concerning this predicament and could only do what he thought would help at the time, that in his mind was to take John out and get him to enjoy himself for just a few hours. Maybe this would help a little bit. Looking at John's face, he knew that it would take a miracle to cheer him up, but he would try his best. After all, what are best mates for?

The show was comical and John did feel somewhat better, even laughing with Peter at some of the skits, and by the end of the evening he thanked his friend for a great time.

"I should have done this earlier...... to cheer myself up." acknowledged John as they pulled up in front of his apartment. It had helped tremendously, he felt lightened because of the last few hours but he knew that even though he had laughed on the outside, in his heart there was no laugher, and there wouldn't be for a long time.

"Now I want to see you at work next week. Okay, all happy and cheerful, even if only on the outside. Brooding in your apartment will only make you think of Belinda more, and that has to be avoided at all costs."

Chapter Eleven

Peter knew It would take some explaining to his wife where he had been for the last 4 hours, but he was sure that once he had told her about John's dilemma, then she would be fine. Obviously he wasn't going to tell her about everything, that wouldn't be right. It wasn't as though he couldn't trust his wife, he could trust her with anything, he could trust her with his life, but this was a friend who had confided in him and he wasn't going to abuse that trust. He loved his wife more than life itself, but there were some things that should remain between friends. If the time came in the future of telling her about his friend's predicament and knowing it wouldn't hurt John, then he would gladly mention it to Sharon, but at the moment though there was no need. She knew that he was a one-woman man and she could trust him explicitly, so there was no need for her to get a full account of everything that happened between him and his mates. Besides he could always soften her some with a quick shower together before bed, Peter smiled and groaned as he felt an ache in the pit of his stomach and putting his foot to the accelerator he went a little bit faster towards his home. Once he got there, he hastily walked into the kitchen and wrapped his arms around his wife's waist, where she was washing some dishes.
"Hello honey." He said as he nuzzled her neck. Sharon slid around and placed her arms around her husband's neck and let the soapy suds run down his skin, she lowered her head to hers and gently kissed him. That sudden ache in the pit of his stomach raced through the rest of his body causing his eyes to glisten as he swept his eyes over his wife.
"Sorry I'm so late," he spoke softly as she looked up at him. She knew that she could trust him implicitly, he had such love and passion in his eyes for her and that was assurance enough.
"Which friend was it this time?" She queried as Peter grinned and bent down to kiss his wife again. She knew him all too well and as he raised one of his eyebrows and took hold of her hand, he led the way to the bathroom and turned the shower on letting the water splash into the base. Sharon giggled and pulled at the bobble that was holding her hair in place, which let her hair fall down upon her shoulders. She knew that Peter liked her hair like that and as she watched his eyes grow wide, they sparkled with apprehension as to what was going to come off next.

The next evening, when Peter and Sharon were holding one another, warm and content in each other's arms from their recent lovemaking, Peter's mind wandered back to his friend. Glancing over at the clock, he noted that it was quite late. 'What was John doing now?' he wondered and 'how was he coping being all alone? Maybe I should give him a ring.' All these thoughts were going through his mind as Sharon gazed up at her husband. She could sense that his mind was elsewhere.
"Do you want to call him? She said. Peter smiled squeezing her tighter.

"You always know what I'm thinking don't you," he replied. Grinning, Sharon reached over to the bedside cabinet and grabbed the phone, handing it to Peter as she quietly slipped out of bed and went to take a shower. Peter dialled John's phone number and listened to the bleeping sound, engaged. Swearing silently as he put the receiver back onto the hook, Peter knew exactly what John had done.
"Dam that man," he thought loudly as he jumped out of bed and went into the bathroom to talk to Sharon. He wanted to go and see John again and he knew his lovely wife would understand, his loyalty to his mates was impeccable as so was their loyalty to him. When he walked into the bathroom, he could hear the water running from the shower and looking over he could see the outline of her body through the curtain. His arousal stirred and a rush of warmth and desire soared through his body as he opened the curtain and stepped in beside her. Just a quick shower he thought and then I'll go see John.

An hour later, Peter stood outside John's apartment knocking on the door. Amazingly he answered it straight away, John had remembered the banging and raising of voices that Peter had done last time and didn't want a repetition of that again. That was quite a start for Peter as he'd been thinking on the way over that he would have to shout and bang loudly as before. John smiled and motioned Peter to come in.
"How's it going buddy?" Asked Peter. "The phone was busy so I thought you might not want to talk." Peter looked over at the phone and saw that his assumptions were right as John had taken the phone off the hook. "But I came over to see how you were anyway." John went and sat down on the couch motioning Peter to walk over and join him.
"I went for a long shower and didn't want to be disturbed, that's why I took the phone off the hook," John replied. "Sorry about that mate."
"Hey, no big deal, just got through having one myself." He said with a twinkle in his eye, that John picked up on. They both laughed even though Peter's was much more wicked. He felt bad then, as that was the last thing John would have wanted to hear, about his love life, although it was difficult not to remember the warm body that he had joined under the shower spray.
"Sorry pal, I wasn't thinking there."
John smiled and waved his hand in the air as if to say, 'forget it,' he got up and went into the kitchen.
"It doesn't matter Peter, this is my problem and I'm going to deal with it the best that I can."
He filled the kettle with water and proceeded to get 2 cups out of the cupboard.
"Want a cuppa mate?"
"Thanks pal. How have you been this evening, did you do a lot of thinking about everything?"

"Some, but it still seems confusing, I can't get my head around it at all." John poured the boiled water from the kettle into the cups and then went back over to sit on the couch passing Peter his drink.

They sat for a few minutes in silence just sipping their drinks and watching a little TV and although John had got it on the Paramount Comedy Channel, and Frasier was on, there wasn't much laugher in the apartment like there was on the TV.
"When did you realise that you were falling in love with Belinda, in your dreams I mean." Peter didn't know how to broach the subject really, talking about loving a woman in a dream didn't seem right somehow, but there it was anyway.
"I guess from the first time I saw her under the waterfall, but the feelings kept getting stronger and deeper each time. John swallowed some of his coffee and leaned back against the couch, stretching his legs out in front, sighing deeply. When Frasier was finished and their cups empty, John looked over at his friend who had got up to place his cup in the sink.
"Well I'm sorry I can't stay any longer, I'd better be going as I told Sharon I wouldn't be long. I just had to come as see how you were."
John got up and went over to Peter, he couldn't have ever asked for a better friend than this. Slapping him on the back, he grabbed Peter in his arms and they gave each other a quick, manly hug, although it was what was needed at the moment, both men did for a second seem embarrassed about it, just for a moment though. After closing the door, he locked it and went into the spare room as he had done so many times that day and pulled out the pictures of Belinda.

The sun came shining through Peter's bedroom window the next morning, lighting up the whole room with its rays. Sharon was still asleep and stirred a little in Peter's arms as he lay there, thinking and recalling some of the conversation that had transpired at John's the night before. He was going to have to talk to Sharon about this after all. Maybe she could help him to know what to do to help his friend. Peter stroked Sharon's face with the outside palm of his hand, feeling the wanting feelings rise in him once again, would he never have enough of her? Would his desire for her ever lessen, he didn't think so at all. God she was so beautiful. Sharon opened her eyes and smiled. He knew he was lucky, one day hopefully they would have a daughter and if she looked anything like his wife, then he would definitely be the one holding a whip when men came calling.
"Morning," she said. He kissed the top of her head as she wrapped her arms around him pulling him closer to her and letting him feel the warmth of her skin under him. 'This is heaven on earth,' thought Peter. He wished that his friend could have what he had. The love of a good woman, a real flesh and blood woman.

"John is having trouble with some dreams that he's been having." Peter explained to his wife. "I don't know how to help him." Sharon looked up at Peter as he continued to explain all about Belinda and her effect on John. She didn't interrupt him at all, keeping quiet until he was ready for any input she had to offer. She told Peter to let her think about it and he knew he didn't have to be afraid of her judgement of John as he knew that she wasn't the type of person to judge anyone on anything that affected them emotionally. Making some phone calls, Sharon met with some friends later on that day who were into Spiritualism. She happened to mention about dreams and their effects on people.

"Tell me as much as you can about this," they had asked her and listened intently to what she had to say.

Chapter Twelve

While Peter was having his lunch in his office, a phone call was put through to him.
"It's your wife." said Helen. Peter had a quick sip of his tea to wash down the sandwich that he had just eaten and picked up the phone.
"Hi honey," he said. "Is everything alright?" What he was to hear over the next few minutes made Peter jump out of his seat and say something to his secretary about him being out of the office for the next couple of hours or so. He picked up his jacket and slipped it on as he dashed out of the building and drove away in his car.

John was watching a program on the TV, although if anyone would have asked him what it was about, he couldn't have told them. Belinda, Belinda, that name was perfection to his ears. All of a sudden someone was knocking on his door. Whoever it was was going to knock it down if they weren't careful as they were banging hard and loud and shouting as well. As soon as John opened the door, Peter came running in all out of breath.
"Take it easy, mate," said John quite startled at his outburst. Peter tried to talk, but it was all coming out in spurts.
"Sit down and have a drink first."
Peter leant against the kitchen counter, his chest moving rapidly with his laboured breathing.
"John," he said in-between taking sips of water. "Sharon has been talking with a friend this afternoon about dreams, and she works in Spiritualism. From what she told me, these are no ordinary dreams that you have been having. She believes that this woman, Belinda is a spirit."
"Peter, don't tell me you've told other people about all of this." John cried out, feeling a rush of embarrassment shoot through him. Shaking his head he walked away from his friend and went into the living room. John turned to face Peter and with eyes blazing, shouted at him.
"This could ruin my career Peter, my reputation would be destroyed if this got out, as if you didn't know that." Taking a few steps closer to Peter before stopping, he ran his hand through his hair and said with as much control as he could muster at that moment.
"And what do you mean, a spirit? What the hell are you talking about, Peter?"
"Just that…..", replied Peter, then stopped for a moment before continuing on, taking a deep breath. "…..Can I bring someone to see you later on this evening, I think they'll be very interested in what's going on here. I'll give you a ring after tea and let you know what time we're coming over. Is that Okay?" asked Peter.

"NO, I don't think it's okay Peter, I don't want my personal life spread across town, and I don't want you talking to anyone else, is that understood Peter, I confided this matter to you and to you only." He could feel the anger rising up him, making him feel nauseous.
"Look pal, it's okay really, I only talked to Sharon and she has only talked to one other person, it will remain that way, be reassured mate that we want to help you and no one else will be involved at all."
John didn't know what to think. 'Spiritual what,' he thought, 'wasn't that to do with ghosts or something?' He knew nothing about ghosts or any other such matter like that. But Belinda couldn't possibly be a ghost. That was absurd, his Belinda was still alive and in London. If he let this person come around, then they could prove it to everyone that Belinda was indeed still alive and well, and not a spirit.
"Yeah, they can come over" sighed John.

That evening, Peter and Sharon returned to John's apartment with a woman who was from the National Spiritual Society, she claimed to be a Medium. 'Oh God,' thought John, 'what is Sharon thinking, that some ghost is haunting me or what.' They entered the apartment and immediately introduced the woman to him as Claire.
"John, this is Claire, she's been kind enough to come over on short notice to see you."
"Hello," said John looking at her with slight embarrassment. 'What had Sharon and Peter told this woman, is she secretly laughing at me,' he thought. John turned away from them and walked towards the living room, motioning them all to follow. When they were all seated, they engrossed themselves in small talk for a good half an hour, which seemed to relax everyone a little and then they talked about each other's jobs and how their careers were progressing. Claire talked a little about what she did for her main career and John was surprised to discover that she was a nurse.
"I find that being a medium and in tune with the spirit world helps me to ease those, who are ready to take their transition over to the other side more easily. I'm able to help them meet with their loved ones who have already passed on and this seems to give them the much needed peace that is required to leave this world behind." Everyone was quite enthralled listening to what Claire was saying, never before realising that working with spirit could have such a momentous effect on helping people find completion, especially when it was time for them to let go of their physical existence.
"I think that the work you do is a great and beautiful thing Claire, to help others in their time of need, but how can you help me?" enquired John, although he loved his friends, he wasn't in the mood for any company and finding himself getting quite impatient, he really wanted all this to be done with and just go to bed to get some much needed sleep.

"What exactly have you come here for, if you don't mind me asking, because I would like to get this over and done with, so why don't you get straight to the point now." He said, not meaning to sound so nasty and hoped he hadn't, as the last thing he wanted to do was to hurt anyone's feelings.

"No, I don't mind John," she replied softly thinking for a moment before she carried on speaking. "I believe that when someone passes over, they leave a certain amount of energy behind that lingers here on the earth plane. Sometimes when people dream, they link into that energy with their energy and they become connected, their auras join as one. Sometimes they join so well that they reach a point where they believe those dreams to be real, they become confused and can't always differentiate the difference between dreams and reality. That doesn't mean that the person is mad or insane though, far from it. All I do with the help from my guides is to find out where that energy comes from, break the link and connect into it myself with my own energy, this way my guides can send it on its way to where it should have gone in the first place."

John shifted nervously in his seat, leaning forward to rest his arms on his legs. He didn't like the sound of that, he didn't want his dreams to end, and never come back. If Belinda's presence was just a lingering energy from a life that she'd had before, then he would settle for even that, any type of love from Belinda was better than none. Suddenly he was experiencing an alarming sensation surge through his body down into this stomach and setting off warning bells, causing him to take a deep breath before speaking.

"And what if I don't want you to do that, then what?" asked John, looking at the floor knowing that his voice had sounded more harsh than it should have done, but she'd made him put his guard up. This was his Belinda he was protecting here and their love for each other. He wasn't going to allow some woman to come into his life and totally destroy the bond that had developed between them. John was totally unaware that Claire had come over to the couch where he was sitting and had sat down next to him because when she touched his arm gently with her hand, he jumped slightly. She felt his muscles instinctively tighten and knew that she would have to approach this subject carefully, especially when affairs of the heart were involved, so she spoke quietly and slowly.

"I won't do anything that you don't want me to do John, but you have to realise that these dreams are not real, the energy that radiates from this woman's past is real, but the actual existence of any love that you have found with this spirit is not and this energy to some extent is harming you." He didn't say anything but continued to look down at the floor. What could he say to something like that?

"May I walk around for a few minutes?" Claire asked. John extended his open hand and nodded to her, making sure that she took it as a 'yes'. Claire got up from her seat and proceeded to move around his apartment.

There was quite a strong atmosphere present in the room making the rest of them sit quietly and say nothing, John could tell that his friends could feel it just by looking at their faces. It was like a sense of confusion, weariness and emotional pain all rolled into one. He thought that maybe his friends were a little embarrassed at all this, but then again they had done this sort of thing before, because he'd heard Sharon talk about it to Peter. Maybe it was just his own embarrassment that was causing this quietness that had entered his home, he didn't know. Claire returned into the living room and sat back down next to John taking his hand in hers, which John held without complaint. When he lifted his head and into her eyes, he could see the love that was flowing out from her. Not the kind of love as a woman has for a man, but the love that flows from one human being to another, letting them know that they care. She smiled holding onto his hand. It comforted John and this made him relax a little, his heart beating just a little bit slower and he could feel his muscles unwinding and the tension leaving his body the longer she sat there. Maybe this was some sort of healing power that she might have as he had heard about that sort of thing too.

After a few minutes of silence, Claire spoke.

"You are surrounded by an energy of souls reuniting after an absent away, there is an abundance of love here in this house," she said. Upon hearing these words John looked up at her, he shifted uneasily in his seat because he didn't quite understand what she was on about. This must have shown in his face, because Claire tilted her head slightly and smiled.

"What we have here," she said, "Is a soul that has just passed over, as her energy is still very strong, but she must feel lost as she is wandering around. This woman must think that she is alive and doesn't realise that she has died. Some of her family is here with her, no doubt trying to help her pass over onto the other side, where she belongs. But like I said, she thinks that she is still alive and some part of her is clinging on to the memories of her life." John felt a cold shudder go through him and he shivered remembering the last conversation he had had with Belinda and her saying that she felt she was alive, but didn't understand what was happening to her. If it was true what Claire was saying, then he would have to let Belinda go and sacrifice the love that they had shared, he felt that was the least he could do for Belinda and for her soul to find peace. His heart wanted Claire to stop, and pretend that she hadn't said any of those things, to pretend that this evening was all a dream, but his head was telling him to stop all this stupidity, and to get on with whatever Claire had to do, for Belinda. But still his heart was screaming out for help, beating faster with every word that Claire spoke.

There was silence for a few moments, and Claire's face grew solemn. She let go of John's hands, quickly stood up and walked over to the window and as she looked out, she appeared to be talking to someone.

This seemed to last a long time, but in reality maybe it was only a couple of minutes. John looked over at Peter and Sharon.

"What is she doing?" he mouthed to them, hoping they understood what he was saying. Peter looked at Sharon and she shrugged her shoulders. They were both as much astounded as John was. Claire turned around and walked back to John and sat down next to him once again with a smile upon her face. Claire moved her body so that she was facing John and looking at him, making sure that they had eye to eye contact.

"John, does this woman stay with you all the time in your dreams?" She didn't like asking John questions. He was tense enough as it was and he looked very drained, but she had to have some answers. She could see that his face was pale and his eyes looked empty. She knew that he was frightened at the prospect of losing Belinda's love and her soul and knowing that if that happened, he might lose his also.

"Most of the time yes," John answered her. "Why does that matter, since Belinda is just some lingering energy now, it is not important any more?" John stood up and walked over to the kitchen.

"This is getting too much. I don't understand any of this, it's just confusing me even more." He shouted as he poured himself a drink, turning around offering the others one. When everyone was settled back in the living room with their drinks, John took his place again next to Claire. She took his hand and held it between both of hers like she did before, sensing that he needed some sort of human contact to see him through this.

"John, I'm only human and sometimes when I link with my guide, I don't always get it right. My guides are telling me that she is very much alive, as much as you, me, Peter or Sharon here so I don't think Belinda is dead...........I thought she was, but......" John turned his head and stared at Claire. 'What the hell was she talking about? Was she just trying to confuse him even more? He had just finished telling her that she was confusing him, how was this supposed to make things any clearer? Of course Belinda wasn't real, two minutes ago, she was saying how she was nothing more than some energy.

"What are you talking about, Claire, you know very well that I have only seen Belinda in my dreams, and you said so yourself, that Belinda is a soul lost and wandering." He pulled his hand free from Claire and stood up.

"This is getting ridiculous, what game is this woman trying to play here," waving a hand towards Claire, whilst looking at Peter for some kind of support. He turned abruptly around to face Claire, shaking from head to toe.

"This is my heart you're toying with here Lady." Seeing the look on everyone's faces, he suddenly realised that he had raised his voice more than he had ever done with a woman, surprising himself so much that he couldn't apologise quick enough afterwards.

"I'm sorry Claire, I don't know what's come over me lately," he said rubbing his brow with his fingers.

His headache was getting much worse and the room was starting to spin so quickly that he went and sat back down next to Claire. Leaning back against the couch with his eyes shut, he heard her talk again.

"I'm the one who's sorry John, I should have talked more with my guides before blabbering on about energies and so forth. This has been a lesson for me too, to converse with my guides before I open my big mouth so I know exactly where everything fits in before talking. I didn't ask for an explanation beforehand because I've seen this before and I assumed incorrectly that you were in the same situation. My guides' let me waffle on knowing that I would stumble and have to find the right answers myself by asking them eventually. The last time this happened, it was exactly as I had said, but this is different and I should have known not to take anything for granted. No two situations are the same and I can't apologise enough for any more pain I may have caused you."

She got up and asked to be excused for a few minutes and explained that she needed to go to the bathroom, not letting them know that she actually needed time to compose herself once again. To get control of the situation and calm herself down. She returned back to the living room within minutes and took her place next to John.

"You two are in limbo, different types of limbo, but nevertheless, both your souls have been searching for that infallible something. When you united together in your dreams, you're souls were joined as one and it's as if you both had come home." Claire continued to speak, but John couldn't take in much of what she was saying. Something about him and Belinda being out of their bodies, astral projecting and John has been helping Belinda somehow. This was all getting too much for him.

"I can't listen to any more of this tonight, my mind isn't working and I can't get my head around any of this," he said as he quickly stood up. He didn't know if it was because he had stood too quickly or from the lack of sleep and food, but his body gave up and he collapsed onto the floor. Peter rushed over.

"John mate," he said assessing his friend, checking him for his pulse and trying to get a response from him.

"Sharon, call the ambulance now." Looking up at Sharon, he hoped she hadn't noticed the slight quiver in his voice.

Chapter Thirteen

They had all managed to get John into his bed by the time the ambulance arrived. The Paramedics checked him over saying that he was OK and didn't need to be taken to casualty, but he was quite malnourished and thoroughly fatigued as if he hadn't slept or eaten properly in days. All he needed was some good food and a good night's sleep. Claire thanked them as they left and went back into the living room to where her friends were standing.
"I think we should ask John to come and stay with us for a few days, don't you think darling?" said Sharon.
"You're right love," replied Peter sitting down on the couch before he fell down. This had been quite unnerving to say the least.
"At least that way, you both can make sure that he eats properly can't you?" Claire stated looking at Sharon who had also gone quite pale. They all decided that this was to be the next course of action to help their friend, but they also knew how stubborn John was so just to be on the safe side in case he wouldn't come with them, Peter went out to buy in some food to fill up his pantry whilst he slept. When Peter had left and while John was sleeping, Sharon took Claire to one side.
"What did you mean when you said Belinda was alive like us?" she probed, needing to know some answers just as much as any of them.
"I believe somehow, only by what I have been told by my guides you understand," answered Sharon, "that Belinda is alive but wandering around outside of her body, searching for something, but I don't know why she is doing this. That's all I can say, I wish I had all the answers, but I don't." And taking her leave after saying goodbye to Sharon, Claire left John's apartment. Claire couldn't tell John any more than what she'd said that night, so she decided not to go back to see him as she didn't want to upset him any more than he was. She knew that this was not the end of it though, because she felt deep down that John and Belinda would love again. That they were meant to be together, they were soul mates.

John had the most unusual dream. He was aware that in his dream, he was a little boy again and was sat on his Grandma's knee in her kitchen with the smell of chocolate cake surrounding them and wafting through the air. He was smiling up at her and she was holding onto him with her arms wrapped tightly around his little body. She didn't talk to him, but just smiled and kissed the top of his head and it brought back all the memories of his childhood, good memories when he would visit his Grandma every Saturday with his parents. The smell of lavender was also always strong in the air as she used it in her baths, saying that it eased her aching bones, this also being the scent of the soap that she used. It was wonderful to bury his head in his Grandma's chest and take a deep breath as this was the time when he had felt the most secure when he was a small child, being with Grandma.

He would sit on her knee all the time while she read him a story and she would always make those fantastic chocolate buns just before he came. John was always allowed to ice them with lots of chocolate butter icing and inevitably was the lucky one who licked the bowl afterwards. He would sometimes, if he was lucky and had been extra good at home, spend the night at Grandma's and when he had retired to bed, after much pouting to stay up with her, she would light an incense candle at the bottom of the stairs, his favourite scent being Jasmine. The aroma would creep its way up the stairs into his room, which he could remember now very clearly because when that happened, he would smile and roll over onto his side, relishing the thought that his Grandma was close by and loved him, with no questions asked. She had hurried into his bedroom one night after he'd had a particularly bad dream. She had placed her arms around him and rocked him back and forth. She had wiped his tears from his cheeks and gathered him up into her arms, carrying him off to sleep with her. Granddad had died a couple of years before, but he could still see evidence of his existence in that room. His tobacco pipe lay on the dresser with his glasses close by and some of his after-shave was still in the bathroom. As he lay there, snuggled up in her arms, she sang songs to him, to lull him back to sleep. In-between singing, she had told him lots of stories and his favourite one being brought back into his mind now.

At the beginning of time
Everyone was born with 4 legs, 4 arms and 2 heads.
The Gods got angry with man throwing thunderbolts at them
splitting everyone in two.
Each person having 2 legs, 2 arms and 1 head,
yet the detachment left the separated sides
with a frantic desire to be re-joined together
as each shared a matching soul,
and ever since then
all people's lives are consumed by
pursuing the lost part of their soul.

He woke up and upon looking around, saw that it was dark, someone had closed his curtains and he was in his own bed. It was during the day though, because he could see the streams of light coming through a slight gap in his curtains in the middle. He looked over at the clock on his bedside cabinet and saw that it was 8.30 am, he had slept all night and hadn't woken up once. Had that dream been a coincidence brought on by the events that were happening in his life or had he been meant to recall that memory. Remembering those words that his Grandmother had said to him on that night, John wondered if that was what was happening here, not that him and Belinda had actually been split in two, but that they were soul mates looking for each other like Claire had said.

John got out of bed and put on his robe and as he walked into the living room, he found Peter asleep on the couch, with one of his arms stretched out over the side nearly touching the floor and one of his blankets from his linen cupboard thrown over him. John went into the kitchen and filled the kettle with fresh water before plugging it in, this awoke Peter who sat up looking around.
"Morning Buddy," said John. "Thanks for staying last night, but really there was no need."
"What did you expect me to do, pal, seeing you drop to the floor like that, there was no way I was going anywhere until I knew you were all right. You sure did scare the hell out of me and the women last night pal." John looked over at Peter and felt his face redden. Quickly looking away he knew he shouldn't feel embarrassed about it, but he did.
"Yeah well, thanks anyway mate," he replied and made them both a drink of coffee.
"Here you are," said John handing Peter his cup. "I'll ring up Sharon and apologise later, maybe she could tell Claire I'm sorry too."
"That would be good, but how do you feel this morning anyway?" enquired Peter, as he took a sip of his drink although he could tell that John felt better than he did last night as he'd got some colour back in his cheeks.
"I'm feeling a lot better now thanks," replied John as he sat in one of the chairs, noting that Peter had relaxed somewhat seeing him walking around looking more like a human being this morning.
They both talked about what Claire had said the night before, but Peter seemed just as confused about what she was on about just as much as he was.
"Sharon and I want you to know that you're very welcome at our place if you'd like to come and stay for a while."
"Thanks, but no I couldn't impose on you like that, anyway I'm fine here."
"Oh yeah, we can see that," smirked Peter letting John know by the expression on his face that he had better make himself healthier quick smart or the both of them would be over and march him off to their place in no time.
"Come on mate, just for a couple of days. I'll get a hard time from the misses if I don't bring you home with me and you know you like Sharon's cooking."
"Ah, you can't bribe me with a good meal, although it is very tempting," smiled John, remembering the last time he'd had a meal over at their house, she was even a better cook than his mother and that was saying something. She'd laid a full spread out on the table and afterwards, if he remembered correctly, he didn't have to cook for the next week. Well maybe that was an exaggeration, but it came close to the truth with the amount of food he had brought back with him. Speaking more softly he said, "I just wouldn't be very good company at the moment." looking out of the window while he spoke.

"Okay, I won't push it, but you just might get a phone call from an irate female later on." They both laughed as Peter get up and prepared to leave and go back to his wife.

Peter managed to get a promise out of John, that he would eat at least once a day and go to bed early, he felt like a child being reprimanded, but he knew that his friends' both cared about him and were only thinking of his well-being. When Peter had left, John went into the bathroom and turned the shower on, he stripped off his robe and trousers that they had left on him last night and flung them down onto a chair, although they had managed to get his shirt off his back, he was glad that they had left his trousers on. He would have been a little embarrassed the next time he had seen Sharon or her friend Claire, noting that they would have seen him in his underwear. He stepped into the shower and stood under the water, but whenever he had showers lately, like now, feeling the water wash over his body, he would think of Belinda and even if he never saw her again, in years to come, she would always be there in his mind and always in his heart. He leaned his hands against the tiles resting his head on them; he closed his eyes taking in deep breaths.
"Oh Belinda, I miss you so much."
'Come find me.' What words those had been upon his ears, the weight of responsibility was so great on John's shoulders to find and help her, but what could he do? nothing. He loved Belinda and would do anything to help her, hell, he would give his life for her and he knew that. But this was so different, how could he help her if he didn't even know how to find her, or even if she was real like Claire had said and even if he did find her, then what? He got out of the shower and dried himself before walking into his bedroom to put on some clean clothes. He went into his living room and slumped around the apartment for the rest of the week in a daze, eating and sleeping, sometimes not even realising what he was putting into his body. He would look down and see food on his plate and know that he was chewing so at least he was eating. It's a good thing his body went into automatic pilot, because otherwise it would've stopped working by now.

Chapter Fourteen

The next weekend, John got up out of bed and gave himself a good talking to. 'You have to pull yourself out of this mate, if you do end up finding Belinda, what good are you going to be if you're like a zombie.' He made himself a cup of coffee and went for a quick shower and just as he was about to make another cup, hoping it would help him, the phone rang, picking up the receiver, he heard an excited Peter on the other end rambling on about something.

"Calm down, Peter, what are you babbling on about?" responded John laughingly at his mate's outburst.

"John, were you planning on going out today mate?" he asked with excitement in his voice but carried on without waiting for a reply. "Well, don't because I'm coming straight over, DON'T GO ANYWHERE," that last part definitely stressed, with that Peter hung up not even waiting for an answer. What was all that about, thought John? replacing the receiver, never mind, because by the sounds of it, he was going to find out soon enough and he was right. Within 15 minutes of the phone ringing, Peter came barging into John's apartment, not even knocking on the door, good job John had unlocked the door already or the door would have come off its hinges the way he made his entrance. He was clutching a newspaper in his hand.

"John, do you remember when you told me all about Belinda, how you felt about her, but more particularly, you showed me the drawings that you'd done of her?" John thought about when Peter had come over and how he'd tried to explain how he felt about Belinda, now realising that he couldn't control the pain as it wasn't dissipating at all. Just thinking about the drawings which he'd managed to not look at for a couple of days, brought back the distress of the loss he'd suffered. 'I wonder how Belinda is and is she experiencing that loss as well,' he thought.

"Yes, but what does that matter now?" answered John becoming slightly irritated as he didn't want to be reminded of any of this, he had to get on with his life and try to forget about the love that never was, before it killed him. Peter walked over and flung the paper down on the kitchen counter next to where John was stood.

"Look on page 12 mate." He said smiling, his voice all shaky. Giving Peter a look of confusion, he opened the newspaper and it was a good thing he was next to the counter, because a rush of heat came sweeping up over his body and he became light-headed. He had to hold on to the counter for support as Peter came over to him and stood next to him grinning. In the paper in front of John lay a picture of Belinda.

"But, that's Belinda". A look of bewilderment came upon his face as he glanced at his friend for answers to this puzzle. Peter picked up the paper and began to read the article underneath Belinda's picture.

"The Police and Ambulance crew brought in a woman from a car accident on the 27 June," he broke of looking at John, "which was 7 weeks ago mate. She has since been in a coma, no woman matching her description has been reported missing, and there was no identification on her at the time of the accident." He looked back down at the article and continued on reading. "If anyone knows who this woman is, could they please contact the Hayworth General Infirmary, ICU Unit." Then Peter began to reel off some phone numbers.

"She's been in a coma for nearly 2 month's pal, just about the same time as you started having these dreams of yours. Do you know what this means?" said Peter getting all excited and gripping his mate's shoulders and shaking them. John looked over at Peter with his hands shaking as he snatched the paper back and looked once more into the face of Belinda. His mind not comprehending what was going on, but as Peter was ecstatic, he began talking too quickly for John and he found that he couldn't get to grips with the whole thing.

"Peter, will you stop talking for a moment and let me think. My head's starting to hurt." Peter took a deep breath and spoke more slowly.

"When you started having those dreams, Belinda had been taken to hospital after a car accident, she's been in a coma, obviously astral projecting mate, she came looking for someone to help her, and she found you. That's what Claire must have meant by Belinda being alive. No ghost at all, she's been leaving her body, looking for answers and searching for a soul to connect to, she linked with your soul......... to you." Peter smiled at John.

"Maybe she's your soul mate after all, and she found you." Said Peter excitedly. All of sudden, the comprehension of what it all meant hit him at last and Peter could see the realisation wash over John's face. He stared at Peter with his eyes bulging out of his head and grabbed his arms.

"Come on Peter, Oh my God, what am I doing still standing here, let's go to the hospital and see her." John was babbling on at full speed, not even thinking of what he was saying. If Peter had asked him what he has just said, he probably wouldn't even have known himself.

The drive to the hospital was a good 30 minutes, and John let Peter drive as he knew that he wouldn't be able to concentrate on the traffic at all. John was biting his nails right down to the core and he was sure that by the time they got there, he wouldn't have any fingers left, never mind any finger nails. When they finally got to the hospital, they drove to the main entrance and parked there, which they knew they shouldn't do, but what the hell, a parking ticket didn't matter in a month of Sundays to the way John was feeling at this moment. The way he saw it, if the traffic warden came up to him to give him a ticket, he would probably write it out for him and sign it himself. He felt so elated and yet he felt sick to his stomach also, his body being in a mess, emotionally and physically.

"Peter, what if this woman isn't her? What if it isn't Belinda and is someone that just looks like her? If it is her, what if she doesn't want me once she wakes up? And all this has been a figment of my imagination after all? What if........."

"John, shut up," Peter yelled as they quickly walked into the hospital, looking around for the reception desk. John was all tongue and he couldn't think of what he was supposed to be saying, so Peter took over.

"Could you tell us where the ICU department is please?" he asked with such composure, John didn't know how his friend was being so calm, he was shaking like a leaf. The receptionist pointed them into the right direction and they took off down one of the corridors. John's mind was clouded over.

"Is this real or am I dreaming again? Am I about to see Belinda, the real live Belinda?"

"Spot on mate." Peter smiled and put an arm around John's shoulder trying to calm him down as when they had entered a lift, Peter noticed John clenching his hands together. As they exited the lift on the 3rd floor, they saw a sign for the ICU, they entered it and a nurse who was sat at the main desk smiled and looked up at them. Peter, looking annoyingly at John as he took the paper from him, wondering why he was just stood there like a statue and staring at the nurse. He showed her the picture of Belinda. He said that they believed they knew who the woman was.

"Would it be at all possible if we could see her?" He asked as the nurse stood up.

"I'll just go and see the doctor, please have a seat and I'll be right back." She pointed at some seats at the back of them and they went and sat down. John couldn't sit still though and he kept getting up and walking around.

"Where is that doctor?" He said impatiently facing Peter, "he should be here by now."

"Come and sit down, John, you'll wear a hole in the carpet, and then you'll have all those pretty nurses running in here after your blood." Thinking about what he had just said, he grinned. "Then again mate, go ahead, that isn't such a bad idea." Peter laughed, he knew just how to lighten a situation, thought John, smiling. He went and sat down next to Peter and sighed as he placed one leg over the other and started wiggling his foot around.

"For God sake John, keep still will you, the rate you're going, the whole hospital will be thinking there's an earthquake." He chuckled. John pulled a face at Peter, but smiled at the same time.

At long last, the doctor came over and extended his hand out.
"I've been told that one of you, or both, may know our mystery sleeping beauty!" he exclaimed. John stood up to shake his hand.
"Yes, that's right."

"I hope that at least one of you can shed some light on the identity of our dark damsel."

"I think I know who she is, but I need to see her in person. A photo in the newspaper isn't always right, and she could just look like someone that I think I know, and not be her after all." John explained. The doctor pointed the way and walked off down the corridor. John strode off with Peter close behind him. God, his heart was beating too fast for its own good. Looking around he smiled thinking that it was a good job they were in a hospital, just in case he had a major heart attack or something. They stopped outside a door, which had a big glass window in it that made it possible to see inside but as John tried to peer in to see who was in the bed, his view was blocked by a nurse who was stood at the top of the bed in front of the woman's face.

"Are both of you going in?" asked the doctor as he turned around to look at them. John glanced at his friend and Peter put a hand on his friend's shoulder, knowing at once what he wanted.

"John will go in, and I'll wait out here," he said. Then he turned and faced John, "If you need me at all, just give me a shout, OK." John nodded and went into the room with the doctor.

Chapter Fifteen

His heart felt like it was coming out of his chest. 'God what if it's her? What if it isn't her? What do I do either way?' thought John. He put his hand onto his forehead and rubbed it slightly, trying to soothe away the pain as his head was starting to hurt again. The door shut behind them making John jump slightly. Trust him to be so nervous, this was the most important moment of his life, a moment he had been thinking of for the past two weeks and instead of being elated about it, he was scared out of wits. The nurse moved away from the bed and went out of the room. The doctor motioned John over and he slowly walked over to the side of the bed. His lower limbs had worked somehow, but he didn't know how his brain had communicated with his legs to move them. It was the hardest thing he had ever had to do was walk those few steps, because those few steps determined the fate of his whole future. He focused his eyes on the face of the woman in the bed, immediately a pain shot threw his heart and a tear ran down his cheek.
"Belinda." He gasped.

John sat on the edge of the bed and reached for Belinda's hand and as he took it, he held it between his own, feeling the warmth of her skin and the steady beat of her heart pulsating in her wrist. He brought her hand up to his mouth and kissed her warm, delicate skin and how pleased he was to find that she didn't have a ring on her finger, well the important finger at most. How he had waited for this moment and to be able to touch her, real flesh and blood this time and to feel the warmth of her hand in his was something he thought would never happen. He looked out of the room through the glass window in the door and saw the doctor and Peter looking at him. He wanted to yell at his friend, 'Look mate, she's here,' but his voice had been taken from him as a lump formed in his throat, even restricting his breathing as he gasped for breath. Breathing deep, he stared back at Belinda as another tear fell down his cheek.

John sat at her bedside talking to her and holding her hand, sitting and gazing at the woman whom he loved more than life itself. He'd given up of ever finding her after days of showing her picture around, no one knowing where to find her. Didn't she have any family looking for her, where was everyone who loved and cared about her, where were they all? John got quite angry thinking of her being all alone at a time like this, when she needed her loved ones around her to talk to her and help bring her back into the world of the living. Time appeared to stand still right then as he gazed into her beautiful and angelic face, all the memories of their times together came flooding back and all the emotions and all the sensations that he felt pierced John right in the heart.

Peter walked in and stood by the side of the bed.
"Is it that time already?" Time had flown by really fast and John was astounded that he'd been with Belinda for so long.
"Don't you think you should go home now pal, just for a little while and get some rest yourself?" he enquired putting a hand on his friend's shoulder.
"No mate, I can't leave her yet." Peter sighed as he sat down in the chair at the other side of the bed by the window.
"Well at least come and get something to eat and drink, you do need a break."
John turned to look at his friend, taking a deep breath and smiling.
"Yeah, you're right there, I am quite hungry, in fact I'm starving," he laughed as he realised that for the first time in the last few weeks, his appetite had come back with a vengeance and his stomach was screaming out for the substance of food.

John walked out of the room with his friend and strolled over to the nurse's station. The nurse was on the phone talking to one of the consultants, so they had to wait until she'd done before they could gain her attention.
"What can I do for you Gentlemen?" she asked with a gleam in her eyes and a smile on her face.
"We're going to the cafeteria for half an hour so we can stuff our faces. Can you please make sure you contact us if the young lady's condition in room 3 changes at all," requested John who'd cleared his throat before speaking, as he knew from the shine in the nurse's eyes that she was interested in him more than her patients. As they walked down the corridor towards the lift, Peter slapped John on his back giving out a roaring laugh.
"My, my, lad," having an amused look on his face, Peter quickened his step as John lengthened his stride towards the lift, not really wanting to get into a conversation about it. "If it wasn't for Belinda, you'd have pulled there mate, and you could have had your own private nurse to tend to your wounds." John nudged Peter in the ribs with his elbow grinning, because he knew that he was only trying to lighten the mood around them. Although John was extremely happy about finding Belinda, Peter knew that he wanted Belinda to awaken straight away, but the doctors had already told him that it didn't happen like that and it was mainly up to Belinda as to when she felt ready and able to enter back into reality.

The nurses were a bit weary of him to start with, after all a strange man just walks into the hospital, saying that he knows who the woman is in the coma and requests to sit by her every evening. Of course the hospital had done a thorough check on John with his work and the police just to be on the safe side. Everything had checked out and after the first few days, the staff on the Ward became comfortable with John's presence and often would come in and sit with him to give him some extra company.

During the next week, John stayed at Belinda's side, only going home at night to shower, sleep for a few hours before going to work and then straight onto the hospital again. He usually bought some food from the cafeteria with him so that he didn't have to leave her. The first night that he'd left her, he'd rushed home, showered and ate some supper then fell onto the bed and slept like a baby until the shrill of the alarm awoke him, content in the fact that he had found his love.

John thought it better that he went back into work and as he headed towards his boss's office, he passed the rest of the lads, who by now had discovered that John had found the woman of his dreams. Peter had promised him that they didn't know the circumstances of their meeting but that he was in love and Belinda had been involved in an accident.
"Look Mr Brown, I know I only originally wanted to take of a couple of weeks, but I really need to be with Belinda, and I could do with another week off." He knew he didn't really need to plead his case, as his boss Mr Brown was a kind man, a family man himself.
"John, you should know that I value you very highly in this department and if you need time to be with your gal, then by all means take it." Shaking hands with his boss had become second nature to John, as he knew that his hard work for the firm gave him respect from a lot of the department heads, including Mr Brown. John left his boss's office and went to see Helen, she was a dear friend and she deserved an explanation from him as to where he would be for the next week. Maybe it would help if he was there with Belinda, talking to her and just holding her hand, so after leaving his office and them consenting to his extra holiday leave, he stopped off at the nearest florist and bought Belinda a bouquet of flowers. He wasn't much into that sort of thing and hadn't had much reason to buy some before, so he'd left the decision of what type of flowers would be appropriate up to the lady who worked there. John was rather pleased with her choice as he got back into his car with the bouquet laid next to him on the passenger seat. There was a beautiful mixture of pink and white carnations with green fern at the back and Lilly of the valley nestled against them at the front. They smelt divine and his only wish was that Belinda could have seen what they were like and smell their fragrance too, but you never know, that might yet happen.

After a couple of days, Peter and Sharon invited him round to dine with them at their home. So going to the florist once again, he bought Sharon some Roses, just to say thank you really for what she had tried to do for him and for Belinda. Sharon's eyes filled with tears as he handed her the bouquet.
"You've done it now mate," Peter said moaning, "she'll want some from me now." Sharon slapped Peter's arm.
"But honey, you buy me flowers all the time," she grinned.
"Yeah well, you'll want more now."

"Of course darling," she said as she walked into the kitchen to place them in a vase. As they sat down for tea, John tried to listen to what his friends were saying and tried to join in on their conversation, but of course his mind was elsewhere. Belinda, Belinda. His heart skipped a beat with happiness, although it would have been even happier if Belinda could woke up and then they could declare their undying love for each other, but hopefully it wouldn't be too long before that would happen. After the meal, Peter helped Sharon clear the table and put the dishes into the dishwasher before retiring outside onto the patio. Their garden was exquisite as Peter was an enthused gardener and he'd bought a swinging hammock for them all to sit and relax in. Many a time, Sharon had told John how Peter had come out the back to do some gardening and she'd found him fast asleep in the hammock. 'Typical man,' she'd said making them all laugh. It was times like this that John was thankful for his friends, because although none of his family were around, he knew there were other people who cared about him and that felt great.

Every day when visiting Belinda, he brought her something in, even if it was a single rose or a stuffed toy, he thought it might help and to tell the truth, it actually helped him somewhat, he didn't know why but it just did.   One day he actually brought in his portfolio and showed her the drawings that he had done. He knew she couldn't see them but as he showed her them, he talked the pictures through and explained each one in detail for her, hoping that maybe she could hear what he was saying at least.

Nearly a week had passed and as he walked into her room once again, he saw the nurse was busy taking her blood pressure so he sat at the side of her bed and waited. The nurse was one of those who'd talked to her constantly and was in the process of talking to her right now.
"You'd better hurry up and wake up gal before one of us nurses pinch your man here, he is some looker I can tell yeah." With this John laughed shaking his head and as the nurse left, she smiled and closed the door behind him. Reaching into his pocket he withdrew a little box and upon opening it he glanced down at the eternity ring that he'd been out and bought that morning. He wanted it here ready for when she woke up and remembered what they meant to each other, each other declaring their love to one another. But if that didn't happen and Belinda didn't feel ready for any commitment and felt insecure of the whole situation, then he would keep it on him until she was ready for their love to be accepted. He sat on the edge of the bed and showed it to Belinda.
"What do you think love, when I saw it I thought of you because it is an eternity ring and when you wear it, it will symbolise my love for you and your love for me, an eternity of love." 'What if she didn't remember what had happened over the last 2 months? What if it had been all a dream on his part.'

He put the ring back into the box and closed it before placing the ring back into his pocket. Taking hold of her hand within both of his, he closed his eyes and said a little prayer.

Chapter Sixteen

Belinda was in the clearing by the waterfall once again, but this time things seemed distinctly different somehow. She looked around and found herself totally alone, no John to comfort her. She looked up at the sky shutting her eyes slightly to block out the glare of the sun. There were some clouds around but they were brilliantly white and the colour of the sky was a beautiful shimmering blue. She glanced over her shoulder by the side of the river and saw someone walking towards her, thinking it was John she smiled as she ran towards him. But to her dismay, it wasn't John, but that didn't matter so much when she discovered who it was that had come visiting her.

"Colin," she cried out, running towards him at full speed. Not knowing how her legs had got her there so fast. She never thought that she would ever see him again and upon reaching each other, they both embraced with sobs on both parts pouring out from their throats, unable to control the overwhelming emotions that were spilling from their bodies.

"What are you doing here Colin?" She asked, pulling herself away from their embrace just long enough to get a good look at him, noticing a single tear fall down his cheek, before letting her body crush against him once again.

"I wanted so much to come and see you before you go back, love." Colin replied as he placed a kiss on her forehead. Belinda looked bewildered and was going to ask what he meant, but Colin, sensing the need to explain continued on talking in almost a whisper.

"You're time hasn't come yet to stay here, you must go back. There are many things for you to do with your life. You have you own family waiting for you to build down there, and there are souls waiting to join you and be a part of that life."

"I've missed you Colin, couldn't I stay here for a while with you?" Belinda pleaded, aware of the tears that were stinging the backs of her eyes, threatening to spill over.

"There are many people down there that will miss you if you stay, you have only to look around and see the friends that you have." He took her face in his hands and tilted her head so that she was looking at him. "Especially the love that is growing in the heart of a certain young man, what we had was very special Belinda, but the love that will grow between you and this man will be even more special." She grasped his hand and caressed it with her cheek. "You have the chance now to have the family that both you and I dearly wanted, don't let my death leave you with a life without love and companionship. John will love you unconditionally and give you children to love and cherish."

"But who is John, is he really real Colin?" Looking deep into his eyes, she knew the answer before he had the chance to say anything. He smiled at her and nodded, kissing her tenderly on the lips.

"Don't forget that I love you and I always will." Letting go of Belinda's face, he embraced her tightly in his arms, as he knew this was for the last time. Letting her go took all the strength that he had, for he too wished that Belinda could stay with him for a little while longer. He walked back up the path next to the waterfall and paused only to turn and smile, waving to her. Belinda took a deep breath, smiled and waved back, letting the tears run down her cheek. She knew that he'd come to say goodbye and let her go, that was what this had all been about. She still loved him but it was a new type of love now and she knew that she would never let that go, he would always have a place in her heart. She knew that her life was with John and that she had to go back to him, be a part of the real world again. She turned away and heard something, 'what was that?' It was someone talking and calling her name. It wasn't coming from where she was and it seemed very far away. A man's voice, yes it was, but whom? Realisation hit her right in the face and sent a warm sensation exploding through her body. Belinda smiled, closed her eyes and ran.

"Please Belinda," John pleaded with her, "Come back to me, I need you." He leaned forward as he fought back the sobs that were trying to escape from his throat, stroking the side of her face whilst a tear fell upon her cheek. Belinda opened her eyes and looked into John's face and as their eyes met, she whispered his name. He laughed almost uncontrollably for he knew then that that his heart had come home. John stood up and rushed to the door, opening it only to see the doctor already stood there with his hands in his pockets, ready to walk in.

"Well, it's about time young lady," he said grinning at her. "We were all wondering when you were going to wake up and join us all once again." Turning his attention to John he asked him to leave for a few minutes whilst he and nurse examined her just to see how she was. John rose from her side, but before going out, he gently placed a kiss on the side of her cheek.

"I'll be back in a minute, now I've found you, I'm not going anywhere." He smiled, but held back the rest of the tears that wanted to flow desperately because of the bliss that his entire being was experiencing at this instant.

Once out in the hallway, John saw Peter walking towards him, he ran and grabbed hold of Peter's arms, not sure if it was to steady himself, as his legs felt like jelly or because of the excitement of it all, making his body buzz like it was plugged into the mains electricity or something.

"She's awake man, she's awake." Both men embraced, laughing and crying at the same time. John knew that he'd better laugh more that cry right now, because if he started to cry, he probably wouldn't be able to stop himself. Ten minutes later, the doctor left Belinda's room and John was able to re-enter and take his place by her side. The nurse went out to get her something to eat and drink, although Belinda surprisingly didn't feel that hungry, just thirsty.

"This seems really strange, I don't know exactly what to say to you." said Belinda, looking at John shyly.

"I know, the only times we've actually met is in our dreams," said John holding her hand tightly.

"Well, at least it's going to give us lots to talk about." laughed Belinda. John brought her hand up to his mouth, pressing his lips against her fingers slightly, letting her know that he did indeed love her.

Chapter Seventeen

Another week in the hospital was all that was needed and then Belinda was allowed home. She'd told John all about renting the cottage and how thankful she was that she had paid the rent a few months in advance, so John had gone to check on it before she returned there, making sure that there was enough food and essentials for her. He would like to have moved in with her straight away, but although they'd talked and loved each other in their dreams, it felt uncommonly bizarre now that it was all real, and both of them felt uneasy to start with. Hopefully, thought John, that would all change soon, very soon.

"It's a strange sensation isn't it John," she said, "I know that I love you, but I still feel scared and also shy around you."

"Yeah, I feel the same in some respects as well." He knew it would take time and patience for all of this to sort itself out. Both of them had talked to the doctors before leaving the hospital and it had been decided that he should stay with her in the spare room for the next week or so just to make sure she was okay and to think, she only lived about 10 miles from his apartment all this time. They knew that they loved each other and because of what had happened, they needed to be close to each other, they knew that they weren't going to lose each other again, but the need to be close was quite overwhelming to say the least. John made sure that she was all settled in before he approached her with what they should do about their wonderful but yet strange relationship and after a few days, he went and stood by her in the garden.

"I think it would be a good idea if we start again and pretend that we've just met." said John. Belinda giving him an alarmed look, made John decide to rephrase his last sentence.

"What I mean is start again as far as making love together, I don't want you thinking that we have to jump in the sack together straight away." He knew that he could control himself if needs be, but longingly hoped he wouldn't have to wait for very long.

"I know this is all new for the both of us and I will respect whatever wishes you have concerning the sleeping arrangements here. I'll use the spare room for as long as you want me to." Belinda turned to look at John.

"That will be quite hard to do don't you think, because deep down, I too want to hold you close and make mad passionate love with you?" she replied. John's eyes widened and on seeing this, Belinda giggled but carried on talking.

"But I do agree that it would be better if we wait for at least a little while." She had found it hard enough these last few days letting John hold her hand in the hospital and kiss her goodbye without wanting more. She'd remembered every touch, every movement he'd made when they'd made love. She knew he hadn't forgotten that either, how could he, it was so special and she thought it was really sweet of him giving her full control of when they would resume their love making.

"I just thought it would make it easier for you," he said, walking over and standing next to her noticing that she was more beautiful now than in his dreams, if that was possible. They always say, the people you dream about are over exaggerated extensively, but Belinda hadn't been at all. He could take hold of her right now and seize her for himself, but that would make him a Neanderthal, and he wasn't like that, he knew in his heart that she would melt in his arms and let him, but it wouldn't be right as she deserved more from him than being a raging hormonal lover. He cherished Belinda and if it took longer than what he wanted for her to feel comfortable in his arms again, then he would wait, forever if needs be, as he was exalted to the extent of just being happy in her presence, that was enough for now. When he did take her, he wanted it to be so special and that would be when she was ready. He admitted that he found it very hard to keep his hands to himself, smelling her aroma when they kissed, as he could smell her now standing so close to her, their arms were touching sending waves of desire coursing through his body. He had tried concentrating on the pond, watching the bubbles popping out on the surface and the fish swimming around darting in and out of the little current being made by the pump, but, oh dear that was a big mistake looking at water. He had been reminded of their time under the waterfall. Groaning, John turned away and looked into the distance over the fields filling his lungs with the fresh clean air, feeling the warmth of the sun as he listened to the songs of the planet's creatures, enchanting songs which were made in this lovely Summer afternoon. Belinda turned around quickly and knocked into John. Grabbing her arms to steady her, the cravings that had dug deep in his loins arose rapidly and he swiftly brought her close to him and lowered his mouth down upon hers, kissing her hard as he let the desires take over and not holding back at all. Belinda let her body melt in his strong, burly arms and went with the flow, knowing very well where it would all lead, but she didn't care, it wasn't as if they hadn't done any of this before. The lovemaking that was inevitably going to happen would be accentuated by the experiences of lovemaking that they'd had in their dreams. John lifted his head up and pulled Belinda closer to him, letting her head fall upon his chest as his heart beat against her and giving her the knowledge that this heart was beating with love for her and her alone.
"God Belinda, I don't know if I can wait," he said as he kissed the top of her head, "But I will, I promise you that, you mean more to me than life itself." He knew his voice trembled as he spoke but hoped that she wouldn't notice too much, he didn't want her thinking that he was a gibbering bunch of jelly. Belinda raised her head to gaze up at him and saw him smile with unabandoned love that shone through his eyes as he spoke, she knew there was no need to wait.
"Come on,"

    She moved away taking hold of his hand and walked him back into the little cottage, up the stairs and into her bedroom. Closing the door behind him, he rested against it and letting his heart, which was pounding rapidly catch up with him. 'Was this all going to fast? Shouldn't they wait?' he thought, 'but by God he did want her and she wanted him, it was going to be OK.' Belinda stood by the bed and turned around to face John, slowly starting at the top button of her dress. She undid one button at a time, watching the muscles in his face twist with the desire that was pumping through his veins and knowing that with each button, his heart was racing just that little bit faster. Belinda sauntered over to where he was stood and let the dress fall onto the floor as she stopped just inches away from him. John's blood heated up sending a burning sensation through his body and as he closed his eyes, he gulped as the hunger of desire pulsated down into his loins. All she had on was a white lacy bra, which let him see the sweet buds of her breasts straining to be released from their prison and white lacy briefs that barely left anything to the imagination. He swept his eyes over her insatiable, body seeing that she was as much aroused as he was, as he watched her breasts rise and fall with her accelerated breathing.
"Oh Belinda, you're so beautiful, more than I can remember." He took one step and was in her arms, swiftly discarding his clothes as they glided back over to the bed. All John had left on were his briefs and as Belinda slowly lowered them to his feet and watched him step out of them, she noticed how much indeed he did desire and want her. Lowering her to the bed, he swept his hands over her body, feeling the warmth of her skin from her arms down her body to her legs and back up to her breasts. He moaned as he listened to her singing her own songs of love. He loved caressing her body and feeling her quiver beneath him, hearing her moans of desire and wanting. His heart would be forever hers now and now that he had her, he was never letting go.
"John, do you think this time it will be even better." John glanced down at her expectant face, seeing it was pink and flushed with the yearnings of love as he smiled.
"You bet your life on it sweetheart," he said as he bent down and took one of her nipples in his mouth and suckled lightly, making Belinda shudder, raising herself up to him and giving to him completely. She moved her hands over his chest feeling him shudder slightly and felt the expanse of his muscles, very strong muscles that she knew would protect her in an instant. He raised his head and took her mouth once again, pressing his chest against her breasts. Catching his hair in her hands, she gripped the back of his head and pulled him down closer to her, eagerly awaiting the ripples of desire that soon would consume both of them. She wound her arms around his back, feeling his muscles move as he breathed above her.

Rolling her over so she was on top of him, he cupped both her breasts in the palms of his hands as she knelt above him, she lifted her head up and thrust her bottom into his lap feeling his arousal, which was strong and pulsating beneath her. His groans grew louder as she moved her hips against his skin.
"Do you know……… what you do……… to me woman," he grunted in-between short intakes of breathes. How she loved this man and how she relished the power she had over him with her lovemaking, she didn't mean it offensively, but she knew the ability of her femininity and how she could use it to please him. John reached over to the bedside cabinet and took a small foil packet off the top by the lampshade. Belinda reached for his hand and held hers over his.
"Let me," she spoke seductively, grinning down at him with her head tilted to one side, letting her hair fall down over her shoulders and over one breast. His hand was shaking as he gave her the packet and watching her open it to take out the sheath. Belinda scooted down his legs and took hold of his arousal making John close his eyes holding his breath, he could barely cope with her sitting against him, never mind her doing something so personal as she doing right now. His body went into spasms as he felt her warm hands on him as she rolled the sheath down.
"You'd better hurry darling, before I lose control," he gasped. She laid her body against his and kissed his lips, sweeping her hands down over his chest down past his stomach to his arousal, where she cupped hold and sat with his manhood pressed against her inner thighs. Gently letting him enter her, she moved slowly and more deeply each time until he was fully inside her. She leaned over him letting him suckle her breasts as she moved slowly up and down and as John took hold of her by the waist, he helped lift her when she raised up. She could see the muscles in his neck pulsating rapidly and the strain on his face as the tension was building up in his body. Rolling her over onto her back, he smiled down at her as he clasped both her hands in one of his and raised them above her head. With the other hand he began to stroke her body sensuously, letting his fingers roll around the top of her nipples and as he watched the desire build in her eyes, her nipples peaking, hard and rigid he continued to move in and out of her slowly, trying to make this last for her, to give her the fulfilment that she deserved from the man who loved her. He wanted this moment to be the best that she'd ever had. Bending down, he licked the tips of her nipples and flicked each one in turn with his tongue, which made Belinda's body quiver as she sent out little moans of pleasure and calling his name over and over.
"Yes, oh yes," she cried, "Don't stop, please John, please."
John placed his arms under her hips and began thrusting in harder and faster until all Belinda could do was cry out with the demands of hunger that were flooding through her body, giving her the release that she so desired.

John followed her within seconds, as feeling her insides contracting with the fire that had been freed within her and as she cried out calling his name, he was also sent up to heaven and to his own release. Rolling off her not wanting his body to crush her tender frame, he lay on his back, bringing her close to rest against him as he wrapped his arms around her and kissed the top of her head.
"Don't ever go away Belinda, I need you, I love you." Looking at her, he kissed her lovingly, touching her lips slightly with his. Belinda leaned on her side propping herself up on one elbow letting her hair flow over her shoulder once again and resting on one breast.
"You get this straight mister," she said pointing a finger at his chest. "I'm afraid you're stuck with me, I'm not going anywhere." John felt that familiar overwhelming feeling that he'd had during his dreams with Belinda, a feeling of total devotion to this woman. Pulling her close to him, they snuggled up to each other and fell asleep.

The light shone in the window as Belinda stirred in John's arms. Lifting her head to look at him, she thought she was in heaven, waking up to find the man of your life lying next to you was a fantastic feeling, a feeling of security, trust and absolute ardour washed over her. It was funny how she didn't feel tired either considering they'd made love, how many times? 3 during the night and not always in the bedroom neither. Giggling she gently moved out of John's arms and slid out of the bed.
"Not so fast young woman." Her body jumped daintily as her eyes flew over to John.
"You scared me to death, I thought you were still asleep," she said and her eyes glistened as she saw he was staring at her, with his eyes roaming over her naked body.
"And where do you think you're going?" he asked grinning.
"I need to use the powder room," she answered lifting her nose up slightly, trying to look prim and proper.
"You may be excused then," John replied laughing.

A couple of days later, Belinda was sat at her computer and looking through her diaries, wondering how she was going to finish her first story. At the moment, there were so many thoughts going through her mind of other things, that she didn't know how she going to focus back on her entries at all. John had driven back to his place to collect a few things, as she had already rung her landlords and they said it was fine for him to move in with her for the rest of the time allotted on her lease. Hopefully soon, when all the newness of everything that had happened wore off some, she could get back into the swing of things, and concentrate once again on her writing.

Putting two duffel bags of clothes and personal items into the boot of his car, John pulled away from his apartment towards the cottage. he had decided that if all went well for the rest of the summer/autumn and when Belinda's lease was up, he was going to ask her to move into his apartment with him. He could have suggested it to her as soon as he got back to the cottage, but he wanted to make sure that Belinda was content and settled with everything, as so much had happened lately and all that mattered right now was Belinda's happiness.

Looking out of the window, Belinda saw his car pull up and watched as his long, muscular legs lifted his body out of the front seat of the car. He strode over to the boot and took out a couple of duffel bags and as he glanced over at the window and smiled at her, she walked swiftly to the front door and opened it. John let the duffel bags drop to the floor as he took her in his arms and swung her around, kissing her at the same time. It would seem that laugher would be ringing out of the little cottage for some time to come now.

Chapter Eighteen

Belinda managed to get quite a lot of her writing done over the next couple of weeks, considering the distraction of a full blooded male walking around. Particularly as he usually wore nothing but shorts and being able to see his muscles rippling as he walked and that smile of his, well it sent shivers of carnal passion vibrating through her. Luckily she was alone most of the time during the day, in body anyway, but sometimes especially after a good night of loving, her mind had been elsewhere and it definitely wasn't on her stories. On one particular evening when John had come home and seen Belinda still working at her computer, he watched her face tighten as she let her head fall to the side and rotate it around to unleash some of the tightness that had built up in her shoulders. He strode over to her and took her hand, she didn't object as he led her to their bedroom and laid her on the bed. Kissing her delicately on the lips, he appreciated the passion that was starting to rise up in him, but he gave himself a stern talking to and held it at bay, not wanting his craving to spoil what he had planned. He gently unbuttoned her blouse but being careful not to touch her breasts, as he didn't want to flame up his desire for her even more than it was already, or her for him at this particular moment. He turned her gently over onto her stomach and pulled her blouse down over her shoulders, discarding it onto the chair. Belinda felt him unhook her bra and then nothing. She knew that he had moved off the bed so she glanced up and looked around seeing that he'd left the room as well. Looking down onto the bed, she saw that she was laid on a towel, which John must have placed there before bringing her up. When he returned into the bedroom, she greeted him with a puzzled look on her face but in return, he smiled and told her to relax and close her eyes. She lay her head back onto the bed and sighing deeply, doing as she was told, she closed her eyes and tried to relax, her breathing being soft and steady. What was that smell, she breathed in a touch of lavender that was floating in the air and John's hands had begun to stroke her shoulders, his hands were all slick with lubrication, lavender oil of course. Smiling she knew this was going to be heaven, Belinda's heart leapt again. What else would John surprise her with in their time together? There was always something that she would never have thought of and this was one of them. Tears threatened to fill her eyes because of the love that was being showered upon her, but she took a deep breath instead to savour the moment. Kneading her muscles with his hands, his fingers slid over her skin and he worked his way down from her shoulders, down her spine and around the sides of her back. Unzipping her skirt she raised herself up a little so he could slip it down her legs, taking her panties with it. He poured more oil onto his hands and began working on her derrière, sliding his hands up and around her waist, then back down her lower back to her rear and down her legs. Before she knew it, he had turned her over discarded her bra and was working her arms and shoulders.

He would have to be very careful not to touch any of her intimate parts, because if he did that, he knew that he would lose control. It was bad enough now anyway, because his arousal was straining his trousers as it was and he was becoming very uncomfortable so quietly he lowered his zip, just enough to let his passion breathe a little. This time was for Belinda and he wasn't going to let his bodily needs spoil it for her. He poured the oil on her belly, making her laugh a little, but when he touched her and rubbed the oil up over her breasts, she gasped with the pleasure that was coursing through to her core. When she looked up at John, he was smiling, but she could see how hard this was on him as well. She could see the desire swelling up in his face as his breathing became harsher and deeper and she was well aware of the electrical energy that was increasing around them. John breathed in deep spurts as he poured more oil into his hands.

"Turn over Belinda," he whispered breathlessly as if saying it any louder would have been too hard for him, his voice obviously being strained. She slowly turned, making every movement erotic and seductive, she knew she shouldn't tease him like this, but she couldn't resist the temptation. John's heart nearly jumped out of his chest. 'Bloody hell, what's she doing, this is unbelievable.' She was only turning over, but he wanted to climb into the bed with her and take her right then and there. "No," he muttered to himself because he'd made a promise to himself, this was Belinda's time. He continued to work on her shoulders and could feel Belinda's body relaxing more and more under his hands, her breathing slowed down and her eyes closed once again. John knew the minute she had fallen asleep, but he carried on working the muscles in her shoulders and her back for a few moments more. He grabbed a cloth that he'd brought in with the oils and wiped his hands before placing a kiss lightly on her cheek as he covered her with a sheet. He walked over to the door and looked back at his sleeping love, how his heart was bursting with the love that it contained for the woman lying there. He flipped the light switch off and left the room, closing the door quietly behind him. He'd better go and take a cold shower, because although lovemaking had been pushed to the top of his list of things to do, right now was not the time.

When Belinda awoke, she found herself alone, with only a sheet covering her. She glanced around noticing the room was dark and glancing over at the clock, she found it late into the evening. Getting up, she noticed her muscles in her shoulders didn't ache any more and she smiled as she remembered what her loving man had done for her. He was definitely one of a kind that one and she had him, he was all hers heart and soul. With those happy thoughts flowing through her mind, she quickly showered and dressed before going downstairs to find him in the back garden lying on the lounger reading a book.

"Hi," he said as she reached down and kissed him full on the lips. John pulled her down on top of him and sat her on his lap.

"Wow, if that's what I get when you've taken a nap, then you can take one every day." He said grinning at her. Her hair fell upon his chest and he wound his fingers in the strands, feeling the softness and bringing them to his face so he could smell the fragrance of her shampoo.
"Hmm lovely,"
She stretched her body out beside him, draping one arm and leg over his body. She had put some shorts on and John slipped his hand down from her thigh to her knee.
"That was wonderful what you did upstairs, where did you learn to do that sort of thing."
"I watched the film 'First Sight,' although the man in the film didn't do quite as much as I did." Belinda laughed.
"You are the most wonderful man I've ever known," she whispered in his ear.
"Yeah, I know," he chuckled back. They both lay on the lounger and took in the cool night air. "Pity we don't have a hammock," John said. "I'd love to get tangled up in knots with you,"
and they both laughed.

The next day when John arrived back home from work, Belinda had prepared a scrumptious meal of salad, chicken and rice with garden peas and for desert strawberries and cream. After such a delicious feast, John relaxed back on the couch stretching his legs.
"You know what I miss about not dreaming of you anymore?"
Belinda walked into the living room and sat down curling up next to him.
"What?" she asked curious of what he might say.
"The waterfall, and what we did under it," he turned to look at her grinning.
Belinda took John by the hand and this time, she led him upstairs. But not into the bedroom, this time she led him into the bathroom. Opening the shower curtain, she turned on the shower spray.
"We can always make believe," she said as she unbuttoned his shirt and slid it off his shoulders, letting it fall onto the floor. They undressed in record time, leaving their clothes in a heap on the bathroom carpet and stepping into the shower, they closed their eyes as they replayed the time of their lovemaking in the waterfall. Never again would Belinda have to look for someone to love her in that most special way possible, as that unique someone was now stood right beside her.

They both took a few days off from their daily lives and drove down to London as Belinda had an important meeting with her agent. Her agent knew that she would need an extension on her time to finish her stories, but she'd said that she couldn't see a problem with that, but she still had to go and see her though. Her agent was very good at her job and liked to see her clients from time to time in person, so a dinner reservation was made in the same restaurant that John and Belinda had first laid their eyes on each other. But this time they were going there as a couple.

Belinda had also agreed to meet up with all her friends for a few hours the next night and she definitely looked forward to introducing 'the hunk' of the evening that entertained their thoughts a few months back. Belinda and her friends agreed to meet up in one of the local pubs that they used to use and their eyes nearly popped out of their heads when she sauntered in holding hands with John. That particular memory will last with her forever.

There was one place though that she wanted to take John to before they drove back to their little love nest in the country and that was Colin's grave. Belinda held a bouquet of flowers in her lap as John drove to the cemetery, but when she went to get out of the car, she realised that she'd hardly thought about Colin since she awoke from her coma. She wasn't sure whether she should feel guilty or not, but she knew that she didn't. 'Was that good or bad?' John held her hand as they walked down the path towards Colin's grave. Stopping before they got there, Belinda put her arms around John and looked into his eyes.
"Thanks for coming John," she hugged him close to her, feeling secure in his arms.
"I wanted to come," said John, "We both have to thank Colin for what he did." Belinda had told John all about Colin and her conversation with him just before she woke up from her coma. Belinda nodded and they continued on until they stood at his graveside. Belinda bent down and placed the flowers on the grave, giving a silent thanks for what he had done for both of them and letting him know that they will always think of him and never, ever forget him.

As they drove back to their little cottage, Belinda felt tears fall down her cheek. Of course her beloved John noticed her tears and he placed his hand onto her lap, gathering up her hand and brought it to his lips, hoping he could kiss her pain away.
"I love you," he said, hoping it was okay to profess his love to her at this fragile moment in time.
"I love you too," she looked at him and smiled, clasping her hand tightly in his. He brought her hand down and rested it on his thigh and that's where it stayed the rest of the way home.

Time passed very quickly and before they knew it the little cottage was handed back to its owners and whilst Belinda wished them well, she regretted having to hand back the keys. She climbed into the removal truck with John that they'd hired and headed back to his place.
"Do you realise, that you haven't even seen my place yet," exclaimed John as they arrived at his apartment. Luckily for him, he'd phoned Peter and Sharon to let them know that they were arriving and they'd arranged for a cleaning company to spruce up the place first. Being closed up for a couple of months, the place needed airing, clearing of all the dust and the windows opening to let some fresh air back in, etc.

Whilst John helped the removal men with some of the boxes, Belinda went into the kitchen to put the kettle on. That always seemed to be the first thing that was on the agenda of things to do.

That first night as Belinda sat on the couch watching a comedy on TV, John went into the spare room and reached under the bed retrieving the portfolio he'd placed there before leaving for the hospital that day when Belinda had awoken from her slumber. Sitting back on the couch, he put his arm around her shoulders. She snuggled up close and they both sat for a while, quiet and content in each other's company. Belinda giggled as she watched one of the men from 'Men Behaving Badly' who had fouled again with his girlfriend. Tucking her feet under her legs, she laid her head against John's shoulder, she loved being so close to him, she could almost hear his heart beating and hearing him breathing so close to her made her yearn for a much closer connection that they would definitely share later on that night. He stretched out his legs in front and propped them up on the coffee table, hooking one over the other, laughing along with her as he took a sip of the cool beer that he'd retrieved from the fridge. When the program had finished, they cleared away the dishes that had accumulated in the front room and when the kitchen was spotlessly clean, they retreated back into the living room. Belinda had noticed the folder, but she knew that when he was ready, he would show her what it was.
"When you disappeared that last time under the waterfall, I didn't know if I would ever see you again and I so much wanted to remember you as I'd seen you, that I drew some sketches of you and of the places that we shared together."
"Oh John, that sounds wonderful, let me see," she said sitting upright in her seat and placing her hands in front on her thighs, eagerly awaiting the drawings to be placed in her lap. Opening the folder, he took out one drawing at a time, the first one was of her standing under the waterfall.
"This was to remind me of the first time that I saw you. I thought you were the most heavenly woman I had ever seen, just like an angel." Belinda glanced over at John with a gleam in her eyes as she smiled.
"Were?"
"Okay, are, and always will be"
"That's better," she grinned looking again at the drawing. He had captured her hair beautifully, vibrant and glistening under the sun's rays. Her arms were lifted high above her head, sweeping her hair away from her face.
"The pose that you did so often was what I wanted to remember the most, sexy as hell you are when you do that." Making sure he phrased that one right. He noted an erotic surge penetrating his lower body as he thought about it even now, making him silently groan. 'Calm down boy,' he thought, 'wait until later.' The next drawing he showed Belinda was of the river and at one side a couple embracing each other as they watched some squirrels on the other side playing.

"You remember that?" she said with a bewildered look on her face as she turned to gaze at him.

"I remember every minute of every day that I spent with you Belinda." He said glancing back down at the picture, his voice was sounding quite choked now, these drawings were also bringing back memories of when he thought she had gone from his life forever. "Look more closely, what else do you see in the picture." John was intrigued, could she pick out what he'd put in that particular drawing from their time together? Belinda looked closely and with a puzzled look, glanced at John who was smiling at her.

"Look more closely," he pressed his hand over hers. A smile on Belinda's face notified him that she'd seen what he was on about.

"A buttercup," she giggled. He had drawn Belinda holding a buttercup in her hand whilst she stood in front of John, who had his arms around her waist. Putting the drawing on her lap, she cupped his face with her hands, turning him to face her to let their lips glide together. Her heart began to beat faster.

"Belinda, we're not going to get through the other pictures if you don't quit that," he grunted breathlessly.

"Okay, I promise to behave myself, for now," she added the last part with a seductive tone, which seemed to affect John more than he realised as he had to shift slightly in his seat and clear his throat before showing her another drawing. The next one was of them both entwined together, standing under the waterfall, naked as the day they were born, making love. John was suckling on one of Belinda's breasts and Belinda had her head thrown back with a leg wrapped around his waist. The water was running over them as they leant against the rocks at the back of the waterfall. Belinda glanced at John again, seeing his eyes changing a shade darker with a craving that was sweeping through his body and her stomach churned with a desperate wanting of carnal pleasure. Tears were forming in her eyes and her chest tightened within her, making it hard to breathe. She knew he'd pined for her as he'd told her many times, but never to the extent of being able to capture the essence of their love on paper like he had done here. He gently took the drawings out of her hands and placed them on the table in front. Standing up he swept her up into his arms and walked through to the bedroom, softly laying her on the bed, he lay next to her pulling her close, there they stayed embracing their love and holding on to it for dear life. This was not the time for the lovemaking of sex, but for the lovemaking of souls. The next morning when John awoke, he realised they were still fully dressed. He gently swept Belinda's hair around her ears and placed a kiss on her lips. Moaning and moving on the bed, she opened her eyes and smiled. Now was the time for lovemaking of the sexual kind, he thought as he lay his body over hers and began the oldest ritual of human survival known to man.

Epilogue

"Hi Auntie Sharon," squealed Penelope as she ran into the house, flinging herself into her Aunt's arms. Scooping the small child up, she smiled and gave her a great big hug.
"Where's your Daddy poppet?" Sharon inquired looking over Penelope's shoulder.
"He's getting my bag and Stubble," she answered, putting her tiny arms back around Sharon's neck and squeezing tight. Snubble was Penelope's soft toy, a little white lamb, which her parents had bought for her the last time they had visited a local farm.
"Where's Uncle Peter?"
"He's in the back garden fixing the swing for you darling." Upon hearing this, Penelope squirmed to get down and the little 3 year old ran off out of the kitchen door shouting gleefully. Glancing out of the window, Sharon saw John coming up the path carrying a small carry bag in one hand and 'Snubble' in the other, his face looking rather pale.
"Hi John, how's Belinda?" she asked with a worried look on her face as she held the door open for him.
"Oh, she's as good as one can get saying that she's in labour," his eyes looked strained and his voice was shaky as he set Penelope's things down by the couch before looking over at his friend. "Are you sure it's OK for Penelope to stay for a couple of days?"
"Don't be daft, of course it is,"
"Well, I'll pick her up as soon as the baby is born and settled into the nursery at the hospital. And don't forget, she can't sleep without a night light, I've put one in her bag just in case you didn't have one and she likes to have Snubble with her as well." Sharon said she knew all about little Penelope's sleeping arrangements as she and Belinda had talked about it enough. Scurrying him off down the path and into his car she waved to Belinda who was sat in the front of the car. She gave a comforting smile and Sharon could tell that it was through clenched teeth, as they backed out of the driveway and drove off. Sharon went to the back door of her kitchen and saw that Penelope had sat on the swing already with Uncle Peter pushing her. How she wished that she could tell everyone that she and Peter were to have a little bundle of joy themselves soon, but they had decided to wait until after the dreaded 3 month period, just to be on the safe side as she had already suffered two miscarriages and didn't want to tempt fate. She was already 9 weeks now, so maybe, if Peter agreed, maybe they could just temp fate with John and Belinda and tell them after their baby was born, she did so much want to tell her dearest friends about their good fortune. Maybe when John came to pick up Penelope and they went with him to see Belinda and the new baby. She would talk to Peter about it after tea.

Even though Belinda had given birth to Penelope and John had been there to witness his daughter's birth, he was still looking quite pale when she was wheeled into the delivery room and he was whisked away to be gowned. He remembered the first time with Penelope, when Belinda woke him up at 2 o'clock in the morning, telling him that her waters had broken, he had nearly fainted that night because things had started progressing rather fast after that. The midwife had called for an ambulance and told John not to drive her, as her contractions were very close together. He'd gone into the bedroom where Belinda was and had sat on the edge of the bed, taking her hand and she could feel his hands were cold, no doubt with fright.
"Don't worry darling," she had said trying to reassure him everything was OK. When the paramedics put her into the ambulance, he'd taken his place at her side and watched as the midwife, who'd come along for the ride just in case she was needed real quick, had put a catheter into Belinda's arm. Belinda had said later that he'd gone as white as a sheet and once they were in the delivery room, his heart had been pounding twenty to the dozen as he'd looked at Belinda's face and seen the pain that she was going through. He'd found it quite hard to keep standing up at the side of the bed as his legs had begun to give way by then. He had never felt to relieved as when a nurse had brought over a chair for him to sit on. When the time had come closer for their first child to be born, John had held her hand and watched the miracle of a new life enter this world.

Now it was happening again, but he was more prepared this time. Talking softly and soothing Belinda's brow with a cool cloth, he tried to help his wife through this hard but yet glorious time, even though his heart was once again beating twenty to the dozen.   After what seemed like forever, Belinda and John were looking down at their newborn son.
"He's perfect," said John with a lump in his throat, sitting down on the bed next to Belinda as he touched his son's hand with one of his fingers. Tears were threatening to flow, but he sniffled instead and kissed his wife, although Belinda did notice one stray tear fall down his cheek.
"What are we going to call him,"
"I don't know, everything we think off doesn't seem right, does it?" smiled Belinda.
"What about after your dad," said John, he knew that Belinda had loved her parents and he thought Craig sounded just right.
"Oh John, I do love you," she said as she pulled him closer for another kiss. Just then a nurse walked into the room.
"Just come to check up on the new arrival and his mum." She took out a funny looking contraption that John knew was for checking blood pressure and moved away from the side of his wife so that the nurse could do her job properly.

"And how's the proud father of this fine looking boy," the nurse said glancing over at John who all of sudden was standing up straighter and feeling pleased as punch with a big grin on his face.
"Well I'd better go and get Penelope, she'll want to come and say hello to her new brother." He kissed his wife once more and left the hospital. Driving back to his friends, he thought back to 5 years ago when he'd first noticed Belinda in the restaurant. He knew then that he was attracted to her, but he would never had imagined the turn of events that would lead them to having a family together.

Once he arrived back at Peter's and Sharon's and after being congratulated and having had several slaps on the back, John seated Penelope into her car seat with Sharon seated next to her. Peter went in the front with John as they drove away, all eager to meet the latest member to the family. Once they got there, John sat beside Belinda on the bed, whom still held their son in her arms and Penelope sat on her dad's knee. Peter jumped up from the chair by the side of the bed and went over to his coat, getting something out of his pocket.
"Smile everyone," he said, as they looked around and smiled, a flash lit up the room making little Craig squirm. That was one picture that would be treasured for years to come, something that could be shown as evidence of their perfect little family.
"We have some news for you," said Sharon smiling as Peter came over to her side and placed an arm around her waist.
"We're going to have a little addition of our own soon." There were congratulations all around as John said.
"You'd better keep that arm where it is for a while mate and remember what it feels like, because pretty soon, you won't be able to do it." Belinda thumped him on the arm and pulled a face. They all laughed.
"I tell you what mate," said Peter, "I can't wait to see what it feels like when she gets big, I bet it's wonderful."
"That it is, pal, that it is," stated John looking at his wife with a tremendous amount of love flowing from him. After Peter and Sharon had taken Penelope back to their house, John was sitting next to Belinda on the bed watching her feed their son the way that nature intended, with love overflowing from his heart once again, but now there was another person that had taken root in his heart. How there could be any room left he didn't know as his heart felt like it was going to explode as it was.
"John,"
He looked into his wife's eyes and saw them glinting.
"Hmm," he said glancing back down at his son as he nuzzled at his mother's breast.
"I've had an idea for another story that I'd like to write, but first I thought I'd mention it to you, because it involves all of us."
She lifted her eyes from her son to her husbands. He was still looking at Craig.

She lifted her free hand and tilted his head so he was looking at her. Smiling at him she told him of her plan to write about their experiences whilst they were dreaming.
"That's a great idea," he stated but then looked seriously solemn, "as long as you change names and places like you did with the others." He didn't want any quacks ringing up causing his family any grief, thinking that they were mad or something. She promised that she'd be discreet about the whole matter like she had been with the others.

The first afternoon Belinda had come home with their son, he was in the bassinet at the side of the couch asleep after just filling himself with his mother's milk. John and Belinda relaxed together on the couch with their arms around each other and Belinda's head rested on his shoulder. As usual Penelope was sat on the floor in front of them drawing a picture in her drawing book, she loved to draw and was always asking for more paper or more colours to use.
"That's a lovely drawing Penelope," said John as he glanced down to look at it.
"It's for Colin," revealed Penelope as she carried on with her picture not noticing the confusion in her parent's face. John and Belinda looked at each other with puzzled expression, but it was John who nudged Belinda trying to get her to say something to their daughter.
"Who's Colin?" Belinda asked all of a sudden, as a chill ran up her spine.
"Colin's my friend, I knew him before I came to live with you and Daddy." Penelope answered not even looking up from her picture as she carried on colouring it in. Belinda and John went and sat down on the floor by their daughter and looked at the drawing that she was doing more closely.
"Who are all the people in your drawing darling?" John had to ask because in the picture there was a man and woman with two children by their feet, and in the top corner of the page was a picture of another man who was stood on his own.
"The man and lady who are holding hands are you and Mummy," she explained, "and the little girl is me and the little baby is Craig," she said with a big smile on her face.
"Who's that man over in the corner?" asked Belinda, but before Penelope answered, she already knew what her answer would be, which sent chills up her spine again.
"That's Colin of course silly," with a smile on her face, as she glanced at her mummy as if to say, 'you know mummy!.'
"He's my friend, he brought me down to live with you and Daddy, and he brought Craig too." With this Penelope got up contented that she'd answered her question with total clarity and ran outside to play. As they both glanced down at the picture, they smiled at each other and knew that no words had to be said. Belinda, giving a brief thought of thanks to Colin, reached out her hand to John and linked their fingers together.

Made in the USA
Charleston, SC
08 October 2015